# PRAIRIE GEM

∽⧂∽ *A Love Story* ∽⧂∽

*Dawn,*

*I hope you enjoy reading*
*this as much as I enjoyed*
*writing it.*

*Cheryl*

## CHERYL SIMONS

LifeRich
PUBLISHING®

LifeRich Publishing is a registered trademark of
The Reader's Digest Association, Inc.

LifeRich Publishing books may be ordered through booksellers or by contacting:

LifeRich Publishing
1663 Liberty Drive
Bloomington, IN 47403
www.liferichpublishing.com
844-686-9607

ISBN: 978-1-4897-3081-7 (sc)
ISBN: 978-1-4897-3080-0 (e)

Print information available on the last page.

LifeRich Publishing rev. date: 09/10/2020

# CONTENTS

# INTRODUCTION

The story takes place in Northeastern Colorado where my roots are. My parents were both born and raised in Holyoke, Colorado, and I was born there as well. I changed the name of the town for the story. I have so many fond memories of the area and wanted to share them.

This is based loosely on my paternal grandmother. Her family moved to Denver from Arkansas for her health. She was on the verge of getting tuberculosis and Denver's climate was famous for helping people with respiratory problems. She attended the Denver Normal School – a teachers' college. (I found the letter her teacher in Arkansas prepared for her to present to the Normal School in my mother's cedar chest). Her first teaching position was in Holyoke, Colorado in a one-room school and she met my grandfather there. My paternal grandfather had a homestead outside of Holyoke when they got married. The last conversation I had with her was sort of like the beginning of this story. She told me she had a dream/vision of a beautiful, green garden and that a man asked her to come across a stream with him but she declined and woke up in a hospital room.

My maternal great-grandfather homesteaded in the Holyoke area as well. My grandpa grew up on the ranch and eventually bought it from his siblings. The ranch/farm where this takes place is modeled after my maternal grand-parents' home. The big barn and outbuildings are described as I remember them. I spent a lot of my summers there when I was a child. My maternal grandmother made some really pretty clothes out of fabric from flour sacks using a treadle sewing machine. They didn't have electricity until after WWII and used a wind generator to power their radio and lights in the 1930's. It was not reliable and my Dad talked about not getting to hear the end of a lot of radio programs. Grandma cooked on a wood stove – canning and drying the produce from her garden and meat from the animals they raised. There was little wood – so they used dried corn cobs and coal and even buffalo or cow chips in early days. I remember the harvesters coming through and how hard she worked to feed them – but she had an electric stove and a water heater by that time. She milked cows and raised chickens and once a week took eggs and cream to town to sell at the feed store. She was constantly doing something, even when she relaxed her hands were busy with some sort of craft.

My maternal grandfather was one of six sons. Grandpa and three of his brothers were a rather famous quartet. That's how my grandparents met – my grandma and her father were musicians – playing the violin and the piano at school and grange dances and grandpa and his brothers were singers. I loved to listen to my grandpa and grandma harmonize.

My grandparents' neighbor did not keep his fences repaired and grandpa's cattle got into his field. They lost half of their herd in one day. They were at the county fair when they found out. My grandma's egg and cream sales got them through until they could recover.

I remember my grandparents talking about how hail storms would wipe out one field and skip an adjacent one. They had to deal with tornadoes at times.

My mother and father were both delivered by Doctor Means – I was delivered by Doctor Ralston.

The character Joseph is based on my father. He enlisted in the Navy the day after Pearl Harbor – was tested and sent to the Naval Academy. The things I wrote are based on history and some things he told us. He didn't talk about the war. He did not suffer from PTSD but his war experiences did affect him for his entire life.

When they retired from farming, my grandparents bought property just like Frank and Elizabeth – two city lots across from the city park and near the library, hospital and nursing home in town. They built a lovely home and he was very proud of his yard and garden. When my parents retired, they moved from Denver to Holyoke and eventually lived in the house my grandparents built.

Dad and Mom played Santa and Mrs. Claus for several years – riding in the parade and turning on all the Christmas lights then listening to the little ones' Christmas wishes in the basement of the court house. My dad volunteered at the local museum – which had been the feed store where my grandma sold her eggs and cream. His family had several items on display there. My mom played the piano at the nursing home.

My grandmother was in a club made up of farm wives – it was called the Prairie Gem Club. I loved the way that sounded so I named this little story after it. Hope you enjoy this. Cheryl Simons ☺

# PRAIRIE GEM

Elizabeth was in a beautiful garden. Everything was green and lush. The air was fragrant with the smell of honeysuckle and roses. It was quiet and serene and green – so green. There was a gate at the far end of the garden that led to a meadow. A stream ran through the meadow. It gurgled and splashed as it wound its way along. There was a man standing by the stream. He turned and held out his hand to her. It was Frank, he looked like he had when they first met – tall and blond and young.

"Are you coming Elizabeth?" he asked.

"Where are we going? Where are we?"

"Come with me, the others are waiting for us."

"The others? What others? Wait I have to do one more thing before I go. I'll be back. Don't leave without me Frank"

She opened her eyes and didn't know where she was. She looked around - she was in a hospital room. She was hooked up to a machine that was making a pulsing noise and there was a line dripping fluid into her arm. She wondered "How did I get here? I don't remember being sick."

"Mother, are you awake? Do you need anything? Shall I call the nurse?" She recognized the voice and face but couldn't quite put a name to the person talking to her. Oh yes, it was Charles' wife Laura. She recognized her now.

"Thank you, Laura no, I'm okay, just a little confused, I guess. Where's Charlie?"

"Everyone's in the waiting room. We've been taking turns sitting with you just in case you woke up and needed something. How are you feeling? Are you in any pain?"

"What happened? Why am I in the hospital?"

"You had a fall and hit your head. Linda found you lying on the floor in the kitchen. Apparently, you were on the step stool trying to reach something in a cabinet and you fell. I'll go call the others. They'll be so happy to hear that you're awake."

"I remember now. I was trying to get a vase off the top shelf and the phone rang. It startled me and I lost my balance. I can never get used to that telephone ringing! Well, I'm glad Linda came when she did."

"You're amazing Mother, you truly are. Let me go tell everybody that you're awake." Laura opened the door and called to them. Her family surrounded her bed. The room was full of her children, grandchildren and great-grandchildren. She was exhausted, but she felt well loved.

Her family was reassured that there was nothing more they could do for her and the doctor said that they should all go home and let her rest. After they left, she laid back and remembered her dream. She thought "Why didn't I go with him? I wish I would have gone. There's always just one more thing I think I need to do, just one more chapter in the story of my life….."

# *Chapter* ONE

It was 1904. 19-year-old Elizabeth Ilene Ross looked out of the train window and watched as the world she knew faded away behind her. She was going west, leaving Arkansas and her home for a new life in Colorado. She was traveling with her mother and younger sister Lois. Her older sister, Sarah, had just married and moved to Iowa with her new husband Ralph Elliston. The newlyweds would live with her husband's family until they found a house of their own. Sarah and her husband would both work in the Elliston's dry goods store. Elizabeth envied her sister but was happy for her as always.

Elizabeth's father was already in Denver. He went ahead of the family after he closed his tailor shop in Little Rock and moved his business to a shop in downtown Denver. His letters were full of optimism. Elizabeth hoped he wasn't painting a happy picture so they wouldn't mind leaving everything behind.

Of the three sisters, Sarah was the pretty, vivacious one. She was full of fun and mischief and everyone was drawn to her. Lois was quiet and shy - the baby of the family. She loved to read and would easily get lost in a good book but loved to ride her pony too. Elizabeth was the middle child. She was the studious, serious one, mainly because as a girl she couldn't run and play with the others. She was small and pale and her health had caused the family to leave their home. After her last bout of pneumonia, the family doctor told her parents that if they didn't move from the heat and humidity of Arkansas to a drier climate she would probably end up with consumption and never recover. Now she felt a huge sense of guilt that the entire family was being displaced because of her.

Even though she wasn't as flamboyant or exciting as Sarah or as pretty as Lois, Elizabeth was level-headed and dependable. To an outsider it was apparent that she was an uncut gem that just needed the right something or someone to reveal the beautiful facets within her. To show the world the lovely woman she could be.

The trip seemed to take forever. As they traveled through Missouri and then Kansas, the landscape outside the train windows was flat and boring. There was corn field upon corn field followed by wheat fields with a few cattle grazing here and there on the open range. She missed the green grass and horses and white rail fences of her home. Now, as they got closer to their destination all she saw was flat prairie land with nothing but miles of sage brush broken up by a windmill or a single, stunted tree now and then. Sometimes in the distance she thought she saw riders on horseback – "wild Indians" she wondered? The train was hot and dusty and they welcomed the frequent stops where groves of trees announced their arrival at small towns. People would get off and others would get on and Elizabeth and her sister could get off the train, stretch their legs and splash cool water on their faces. These stops were the only relief in the brown, flat landscape. She wondered what the people that lived in this part of the world did for fun, if they did anything at all.

On the fourth morning of their trip, just when she thought she couldn't take the never-ending monotony of the desolate land another moment she saw the Rocky Mountains. They seemed to rise out of the horizon from nowhere. Their dark blue and purple hues were majestic and awesome, and they were enormous even from this distance. She had never seen anything like these mountains before and she loved them immediately. As they got closer, she could see that there were rows and rows of them that seemed to go on forever and that they were higher than she had imagined possible. Her father was right – this was a beautiful place with lots of promise. She wished Sarah could see them too. Sarah would paint a picture of them or write a poem about them or something that only she could do.

Her mother and Lois were asleep but Elizabeth just had to wake them so they could all share this wondrous moment. Her mother was exhausted and Lois was not as impressed as Elizabeth, but they all were happy that their trip was nearly over.

Her father was waiting at the train station in Denver and the family's reunion was a happy one. He told them about his new business and the apartment over the shop where they would live as he drove the wagon to their new home. Elizabeth hoped this new place would be the answer to her prayers and that she could live a normal, healthy life here.

The sky was such a clear blue it made her eyes water. The air was clean and light – not heavy like at home. She already felt her lungs responding to the altitude and lightness in the atmosphere. "Oh, thank God, maybe this is going to work" she thought. Her guilt was nearly overwhelming at times. Her mother had a haunted look on her face and Elizabeth knew it was because she had left her home, family and friends and the graves of her tiny still-born babies behind. The babies, there were two of them, were not spoken of but were always present in their lives. Her mother mourned them still and probably always would. Lois's eyes lit up when she saw the city – the paved streets and sidewalks and the beautiful buildings. She finally seemed excited and happy or at least not as sullen and sad. She had to leave her pony behind and hadn't let Elizabeth forget it.

Denver was a busy, bustling city with lots of sights and sounds to absorb. After they got settled and rested from their journey the family took a tour of the city. Several years earlier there had been a terrible fire in Denver, causing the town council to pass a law that required all new construction to be of brick rather than wood. The Colorado state capital building was situated on "Capital Hill", a knoll that overlooked the city. It was a beautiful marble building that was designed to look like the U.S. capital building. There was talk that the capital dome was going to be covered in gold leaf to represent the gold rush in the 1800's. The Brown Palace Hotel was right downtown Denver and was the biggest building Elizabeth had ever seen up close. It was built in the shape of a triangle and took up the entire corner of one of the main streets. Her father took them inside for tea in the beautiful atrium area. There were office buildings and department stores, banks and restaurants everywhere they looked. Her father had an agreement with the Denver Dry Goods store to do all of their alterations and so far, he was so busy he'd hired two seamstresses to help. Now that the rest of the family had arrived, they would all work in the shop as well.

After a few weeks her father called, "Elizabeth, come with me. We're going to visit the Denver Normal School." The Denver Normal School was a teacher's college. Elizabeth was thrilled at the opportunity! Her dream was to be a teacher and now that dream just might be coming true! They walked the six blocks from the shop to the college and Elizabeth was able to keep up with her father without any problem – for the first time in her life! She could breathe easily and freely. It was truly a miracle and in such a short time! The school was in a small, two-story building and as soon as she walked in, she felt both excited and at home. They gave the letter of introduction and recommendation from her school principle in Arkansas to Miss Taylor, the head mistress of the school. She was a neat, no-nonsense woman who welcomed Elizabeth with a firm hand-shake and a steady gaze. This was the beginning of her future!

Miss Taylor explained to Elizabeth that her role wasn't just teaching the basics – the ABC's – but that she would have a big impact on her students in ways she didn't realize.

"Always remember Elizabeth, these children look up to you. You are a role model for them and quite often you will be the first person other than their parents to have any significant interaction with them. They watch you and everything you do, so be sure to give them something to aspire to."

This advice gave Elizabeth a different perspective on her new life and she wanted to be the very best teacher she could be. She studied the lesson plans, but also learned about working with children of all ages and abilities. This was going to be a challenge, but one she looked forward to. The curriculum was difficult but interesting. She would be expected to teach a variety of grades and subjects and had to be proficient in everything from English and History to Science and Math and she loved it!

During this time her family made some major changes as well. Her father's business was doing very well and they were able to buy a house on the outskirts of town with a couple of acres of land. Her father bought a handsome buggy and a pretty bay mare to pull it. They named the mare Gypsy and she soon became Lois's companion. Their father hoped that this would be a sort of replacement for the pony she had left behind in Arkansas.

Elizabeth was able to walk the mile from their new home to her school when the weather was good without any problem. She felt better every day – her eyes were bright and her cheeks were rosy with a healthy glow. For the first time in her life she felt good – really good! Her favorite thing about their new life was their Sunday drives. They would pile in the buggy take a picnic lunch and travel around their new home. They drove up into the foothills of the beautiful Rockies that Elizabeth had fallen in love with. They went to the Red Rocks and hiked around the beautiful rock formations. In the Fall they ventured into the canyons to view the autumn leaves. The contrast between the yellow Aspen leaves and the dark green pine trees was breath-taking. And in the winter, they watched the snow turn their new world into a white wonderland.

After two years she earned her teaching certificate and started to look for positions in the Denver area. There was a shortage of openings in the city but there were lots of opportunities in the small farming communities in the state. She wrote several letters of inquiry and soon was offered a teaching job in a town in the northeastern corner of the state, near the Colorado/Nebraska state line.

She arrived at her destination on another train. This time the train went north to Cheyenne, Wyoming then east and south toward Nebraska. She was in a small town on the prairie just like she had seen on her journey west. She was nervous but looked forward to this new chapter in her life. Hartford, Colorado was named for the city in Connecticut and was the county seat. It was a clean, well-ordered town with a prosperous looking business district as well as several neat residential areas and an impressive court house building. She was going to like it here – she hoped….

## Chapter
# *TWO*

Elizabeth was met at the train station by a middle-aged man dressed neatly in a suit and tie. He introduced himself as Wilbur Schubert, the President of the School Board, and stated that he and his wife were to be her hosts for the school year. The employment agreement included room and board with a local family along with a small salary. The Schubert's were influential people in town – he owned the mercantile store. They had three children that would be students in her school. Mrs. Schubert was waiting when she arrived and was as nervous as Elizabeth – if not more so. She immediately showed Elizabeth to her room and let her know when they would be eating dinner. Elizabeth was happy to see that her room was clean and inviting and she looked forward to meeting their children.

She unpacked her valise, washed up using the pitcher of water and bowl provided and went downstairs to meet the family. The Schubert children were red-heads with freckles and big brown eyes – like their mother. Wilbur Jr. or Willy, was 12, Vivian was 9 and Dale was 5. This would be his first year of school and his first time away from his mother. They were polite, clear-eyed and anxious to make a good impression on their new teacher. After dinner, Elizabeth helped Mrs. Schubert (Matilda) clean up the dishes and spent the rest of the afternoon and evening preparing her lesson plan.

Before supper Mr. Schubert took her to the school house so she could see where she would be teaching. It was called Hilltop School because it sat on a little knoll. The building was newly white-washed and was basically a wooden box consisting of one-room with windows on one wall and a blackboard on another. There was a wood stove in the back of the room and a cloak room at the front of the room, by the entrance. At the back of the building was a door leading to the outhouse with a small porch where wood was stored. There were desks lined up in rows facing the blackboard. The teacher's desk sat by the wood stove along side the students' desks. An old upright piano sat next to the teacher's desk. Books were stacked on a makeshift bookshelf according to grades and subject. Everything was well-organized. The school was cleaned and scrubbed and was ready for the new school year to begin.

Mr. Schubert told her that she would have approximately 15 students in her class, depending on the time of year, and that they would range in age from 5 to 14. She would be expected to teach the curriculum for all 8 grades as well as music and art. She was excited – but a little apprehensive too. Music wasn't one of her strong suits. The school year would start the next morning. Mr. Schubert would take her to school along with his children and would pick them up in the afternoon. Willy would be responsible for building a fire in the school's wood stove while she prepared for the day. Vivian would help clean the classroom after school and Dale would help his sister. Elizabeth spent a sleepless night anxiously waiting for the first day of school. She was up before dawn, braiding her light brown hair and rolling it into a neat coil at the back of her head. She dressed with extreme care in her best dark blue skirt and jacket. She was wearing her favorite cream-colored blouse and had tucked a colorful handkerchief in her breast pocket. As her mother always said, "you only have one chance to make a good first impression".

When they arrived at the school there was already a group of children and adults waiting. She stepped onto the front porch of the school, took a deep breath, smiled and said in a clear voice "Welcome to Hilltop School. I am your new teacher Miss Ross! I hope we will have a wonderful year!" With that Wilbur Schubert opened the front door with a flourish and the students entered her school.

There were 10 students that first day and she spent the first hour learning their names and ages and assessing their skills. They talked openly and willingly about what they already knew and with some exceptions they seemed happy to be there. She asked if there was a United States flag and was told that there was one in the storage room and that Walter Bauer was responsible for raising and lowering it. He knew the rules. However, he wasn't there yet – he had work to do on his family's farm and wouldn't start school for a few weeks. A boy of about 10 timidly raised his hand and asked if he could take care of the flag duties – just until Walter came to school.

"Of course!" Elizabeth said. "Do you know the protocol?"

"Um, what's protocol?" he asked.

"You know, how, to fold the flag, making sure it doesn't touch the ground, and that sort of thing."

"Oh yes! I know all about that. Walter is my older brother and I help him."

"What's your name and how old are you?"

"Harold is my name and I'm 11 years old."

"Thank you, Harold. I'm sure you will do nicely until your brother returns."

Everyone seemed to be agreeable to this solution so Harold got out the flag and raised it on the flag pole outside the front of the school. Elizabeth was feeling more and more comfortable as the morning went on. She led them in saying the Pledge of Allegiance and the Lord's Prayer and the classes began.

Later in the morning she called "Its recess time!" The boys and girls jumped up from the desks and started running to the front door.

"Whoa! Hold on! Line up and take your time. We don't want a stampede or any casualties." The kids thought that was pretty funny – since most of them didn't know what "casualties" were but thought it must have something to do with cowboys and Indians and stampedes. Elizabeth was also in charge of supervising the recess activities and soon realized that she would have to come up with some games that everyone could play. After recess they came back into the classroom and after a few minutes of restlessness, they settled down to finish their assignments.

And so, Elizabeth's teaching career and the next chapter in her life began. She thought she was the luckiest young woman in the state of Colorado! The first signs of that uncut gem were starting to show through.

After a few weeks the older kids came to class. There were four boys and they were all bigger than Elizabeth. They were working on their family farms and were ready for a much-needed break. There was a definite "pecking order" and once the big kids arrived, everything changed. One of the older boys was the obvious leader. Everyone deferred to Glen and he took on the responsibility of running things without a second thought. He was a natural leader and that's just the way it had always been and would always be. Elizabeth quickly realized that she had to earn his respect or he would be running her as well. He had two younger siblings in the school and apparently, they had already told him about her and her teaching methods. She could tell he was going to be a challenge.

One morning Elizabeth heard a scream and one of the younger girls came running in from the outhouse, crying. There was a snake hanging from the doorframe and it had dropped down right in front of her, almost landing on her shoulders. Without a second thought, Elizabeth grabbed the hatchet that was used for the wood stove and ran out to the outhouse. She found the snake and chopped off its head in one quick movement. Of course, everyone followed her outside to see what she was going to do.

She looked up to see a cluster of faces with wide eyes staring at her. Glen stood on the back porch of the school and asked. "Do you know that you just killed the best ratter in Phillips County?"

"What do you mean?"

"Oh, just that a bull snake like that kills all the rats and mice in the area and keeps things under control. That was a famous snake. Everybody knew that snake and now you've killed it."

"Well, that snake's killing days are over. Maybe we should just hire a cat!"

Everyone thought that was pretty funny – "hiring" a cat? What an idea! The next morning Glen came to school with a cat in a burlap bag. The class named the cat Snake and she kept the school yard free of rats and mice, the little girls weren't afraid to use the outhouse and Elizabeth passed a test. Glen and the other boys seemed to have a little more respect for her.

Elizabeth's days settled into a nice, comfortable routine. She loved teaching the children and seeing their faces light up when they learned something new. The days became weeks and before she knew it, they were preparing for Thanksgiving. The weather was unpredictable so she decided to stay in Hartford rather than go back to Denver for the holiday. She asked the Schubert's what they usually did for Thanksgiving and was told that they had a family dinner of turkey and the fixings. She wanted to have a celebration at the school and wondered if the other parents would like the opportunity to come to a pot-luck dinner. The Schubert's thought it was a wonderful idea, so Elizabeth sent a note home with each child inviting their families to a holiday dinner the Saturday after Thanksgiving. Without exception every family replied with an enthusiastic YES! With her limited resources she purchased a big turkey and she and Mrs. Schubert prepared it for the party.

The party was a huge success. Each mother brought her own special dish. The fathers spent the day eating, drinking punch and occasionally going outside for a sip of something a little stronger while they talked about the weather and crop prices. The women visited and shared recipes and watched the children play including Elizabeth in their group as though she had always been there. Elizabeth was impressed with these people. They were very interested in their children's education and wanted the best for them. They were quiet, unassuming and honest. They loved their God, their families and their land.

As she enjoyed relaxing with her new found friends, she heard a commotion outside. Someone called "The Wagner brothers are here!" Who were the Wagner brothers? Elizabeth had no idea what they were talking about. Then the door opened and four young men came in to the room. Everyone was excited to see them. Elizabeth's heart gave a little jump and she blushed when Mr. Schubert introduced her to Frank Wagner, "the best baritone in the county". He was taller and blonder than the others and was quite good-looking, she thought. He smiled, shook her hand and said "I've heard a lot about you Miss Ross." He had a delightfully deep voice and very strong hands. The women clustered around the young men offering plates of food and cups of punch. They were obviously celebrities in the area. As the day went on the desks were all moved to one end of the room making a clearing in the middle. Soon one of the brothers took out his fiddle and another brother sat down at the piano and the Wagner brothers began to sing. Their voices harmonized beautifully as they sang all the favorite songs of the day. They were truly talented and Elizabeth understood why everyone was so happy to see them arrive. Everyone was dancing and laughing and having a wonderful time. The Schubert's were very good dancers and Elizabeth danced with her younger students while the Wagner's played and sang.

While everyone cleaned up after the party Frank Wagner approached Elizabeth. "I hope you enjoyed our singing, Miss Ross" he said shyly.

"Absolutely! It was wonderful. But how did you know we were having a party?" she asked.

He smiled and said, "Everyone within 20 miles knew you were throwing this party. Wilbur asked us if we'd like to come and of course, we're never ones to turn down a home-cooked meal!" She liked his smile and didn't want the conversation to end, but didn't know what to say to make him stay. He took care of that problem.

"Everyone's been talking about the new school teacher and how pretty she is, and I just had to see for myself" he said with that same smile in his voice. "They were sure right! I've never seen anyone with eyes that color. What do you call it?"

She blushed again and thought "this man is too charming. I hope he's sincere, because I think I like him!"

"I think they're hazel or green or blue, depending on my mood" she replied. Where do you live Mr. Wagner?" she asked. Then thought, "That was awfully forward of me – I hope he doesn't think I'm desperate!"

He grinned, "Well, you must be in a good mood today, because they are beautiful! I have a little place about 12 miles southeast of town – almost to the Sand Hills. I've filed a homestead claim and am improving the land. I've got most of it fenced and pretty soon I'll start building a house now that I've got the barn finished. I've got a few head of cattle and a couple of milk cows and of course my work horses. I'm a pretty good farmer, if I do say so myself!" He laughed at himself. She liked his laugh and wanted to hear it again.

"What are the sand hills?" she asked.

He replied, "Oh just a little east of my place the land changes. There are lots of hills and gullies and the land is almost all sand, hardly anything grows there except sage brush. Everybody calls them the Sand Hills."

His brother came up to them, "Alright Romeo, let's get going we've got a long ride ahead of us in the dark."

"It was a lovely evening Miss Ross, thank you. I hope to see you again." Frank bowed slightly and shook her hand again.

"You're welcome Mr. Wagner. Yes. that would be nice." She smiled as the brothers put on their coats and hats and waved as they walked out the door. "Oh yes, that would be very nice!" she thought.

Mrs. Schubert said "Well, what do you think of Frank Wagner? He's one of the finest young men in the county. Wilbur thinks the world of him and to tell you the truth, we were hoping that you two might hit it off." She smiled at Elizabeth, "but of course, we don't want to lose our teacher!"

Elizabeth blushed again "I don't know Mrs. Schubert it's a little early to tell, but he does have a lovely singing voice!"

Elizabeth didn't hear anything from Frank and was beginning to think she had been rash in her assumption that he might be interested in her. However, the weather had turned cold and snowy and she didn't have time to think about much other than keeping her classroom warm and preparing her lesson plans. Christmas was just around the corner and the children were hard to control. They weren't interested in reading, writing or arithmetic, just what they might get for Christmas. They all looked forward to Christmas vacation. She tried to make her lessons more fun and interesting in order to keep them engaged. Once again, she decided to stay in Hartford. It was too cold and snowy to travel all the way to Denver so she was going to stay with the Schubert's for the holiday. She had been busy knitting mittens for the Schubert children for Christmas presents and had made scarves for Mr. and Mrs. Schubert. She knew that the children wanted a sled, but Mr. Schubert said he wasn't a very good carpenter, so they would probably be disappointed.

Christmas morning dawned clear and cold with several inches of snow on the ground. The children were all up early running down the stairs in excitement to see what might be in their stockings. Each child had an orange and some hard candy in their stockings which delighted them. Elizabeth had wrapped their gifts in tissue paper and put red ribbons on each one. They happily tried their mittens on and then shyly gave her their presents. Mrs. Schubert exclaimed that her scarf was the most beautiful thing she had ever seen. Mr. Schubert had sent to Denver for a leather-bound journal for her, Mrs. Schubert had made her scented sachets for her dresser drawers and the children each had drawn a picture. Dale's was a picture of a woman and a little boy and said "To the best teecher in the hull, wild world!" She laughed and tried to hide the tears in her eyes. They had embraced her and made her feel like one of the family.

Outside there was the sound of bells and horses stomping and snuffing. The kids looked out the window and called "It's Frank

Wagner! What's he doing here?" Elizabeth's heart skipped a beat. He hadn't forgotten after all! As he brushed the snow off his hat and coat, he shook Mr. Schubert's hand. "I've got your surprise tied to the back of the other horse. Do you want to come out and get it?"

Mr. Schubert quickly put on his coat and went outside with Frank. They came back into the house together. Mr. Schubert was carrying a lovely, hand-made sled. It was painted red with enough room for all three children to ride at once. The children were ecstatic! "A SLED!! they all cried. You made us a sled!"

"Well yes, your father asked me to make it for you. Thank your father it was his idea and his gift."

Mr. Schubert said, "Frank's a much better carpenter than I am so, I asked him to make your sled."

"Thank you, Dad!" they all cried at once. "Come on let's go try it out!" They hurriedly put on their hats, coats and new mittens and ran outside to ride on their new sled.

After the horses were fed and tended to, Mrs. Schubert took Frank's coat and hat and offered him some hot coffee. "You must be half frozen after your long ride in this weather. Please stay and eat dinner with us."

Frank stood in front of the wood stove and rubbed his hands together. "Yep, it's pretty cold out there, and I'd be grateful to stay for dinner." "Hello Miss Ross, Merry Christmas."

"Merry Christmas to you as well, Mr. Wagner. It's nice to see you again."

"Thank you. Oh, I have a little something for you. I hope you like it." He reached into his coat pocket and took out a small package, wrapped in brown paper. It was a wood carving of a deer. It was perfect, with such intricate detail that the doe looked like she was alive.

"Oh my! It's just beautiful! Thank you so much! But I don't think I can accept it."

"Of course, you can. It's Christmas!" both Mr. and Mrs. Schubert said in unison.

"Well, I guess you're right, and of course I love it!" "Thank you again, Mr. Wagner it's wonderful, you are an artist!"

Frank ducked his head "You're welcome, I'm glad you like it."

Later, after dinner the Schubert's discreetly left the room so Frank and Elizabeth could have a little privacy. "How're things on your place, Mr. Wagner?"

"Please, call me Frank, and things are coming along nicely. Pretty soon I won't have to sleep in the hayloft. I'll have the house closed in and can move into it within a month or so."

"That's wonderful! You've built it all yourself?"

"Yes, well, with some help from my brothers. They've all gone to California, hoping to find jobs. I just hope my crops are good and I make enough selling my calves to pay them for their labor next year." "May I call you Elizabeth?" he asked.

"Why yes. That would be fine." She thought, "I like the way my name sounds when he says it" and smiled to herself.

"Elizabeth" he stopped, obviously nervous, "do you think that I could see you again, in a more formal way?" "I would ask your father, but of course he's in Denver and all, so I was going to ask Mr. Schubert if he would agree to let me court you."

"I would like that Frank. I hope Mr. Schubert will agree." She smiled.

Frank started coming to call on Saturdays when he came to town to do his errands. They were getting to know each other and their conversations were easy and effortless. When the weather got warmer, they packed a lunch and drove out to his farm. Frank would proudly show her what he had gotten done during the week and ask her opinion how things should look and on the finishing touches.

After a few months of courting, Frank asked Elizabeth to marry him and she said "Yes!" It was a short courtship, but they both knew that this was the person they wanted to spend their lives with. The next few months were a whirlwind of activity. At the end of the school year she was thrilled to find that all of the children had passed the tests and moved up to the next grade – some even skipped a grade. Mr. Schubert told her that the school board had renewed her contract for the next year. They knew she was getting married but they wanted her to teach for the first semester and then they would find her replacement after the first of the year. She was flattered and accepted gladly.

The mothers of her students insisted on giving her a bridal shower and they each brought lovely, embroidered linens and hand-made gifts for her new home. The students were excited for Miss Ross and Frank, especially the girls. They thought it was so romantic!

Elizabeth went home to Denver for the summer and helped in the family's business. In the evenings she and her mother and sister worked on her wedding dress. It was simple, but elegant and beautiful. She and Frank wrote letters to each other nearly every day. This was Frank's busy time, but he still found a few minutes to drop her a note and let her know how their house was coming along and how his crops were doing. She looked forward to the mail arriving every day.

She and Frank were married the following Christmas eve at Hilltop School, the Schubert's stood with them and all of her students and their families attended the ceremony. Elizabeth's parents and younger sister traveled from Denver for the wedding, bringing gifts and well wishes from family and friends. Her sister Sarah came all the way from Iowa, with her 3-year old son Ralph Junior. Two of Frank's brothers, Ed and Earl, came back for the wedding. Roy, the oldest was working as a policeman in San Francisco. It was a wonderful time. They spent their first night as husband and wife at the Burge Hotel in Hartford. Frank was a considerate and gentle lover and Elizabeth had never felt so loved and cherished in her life. She had married a good man. They moved to Frank's farm the next day to start their married life together.

And so, the next chapter in Elizabeth's life began. It seemed like the right someone had come into her life and that gem was getting brighter and more beautiful every day.

Chapter

# THREE

Frank drove his wagon down the dirt road to their farm with his new wife by his side, hoping that she would be happy there. He stole a glance at her face as they neared the house. He had spent a lot of time and all of his extra money making the house warm and inviting and hoped she would like it. She was quiet and he was afraid she was sorry she had married him. It was bone-chilling cold but she was wrapped up in a coat and hat and had a warm robe across her lap. The cold air had given her cheeks a healthy, pink glow, or maybe it was love. Her eyes were a beautiful blue today.

His brothers had stayed at his place the night before to milk the cows and feed the livestock. Then they plowed a track to the house and shoveled a spot in front of the house to park the wagon. They made a path through the snow to the front porch. He pulled in front of the house and looked down at her. "Well, what do you think Mrs. Wagner?"

"I love it Frank! It's absolutely lovely and this spring when I plant some flowers around the front door it will be even prettier than it is right now."

He breathed a sigh of relief – at least she was planning on being there in the spring, he thought. He got down from the wagon and came around to her side. He lifted her off the seat with ease and they walked to the front door arm in arm.

During the past year, Frank had built a neat little house for them consisting of two bedrooms, a sitting room and a kitchen with an eating area. He had dug a root/storm cellar with an outside entrance to store essentials. Elizabeth's suggestions and ideas had been sensible and improved on his original.

The barn was big and well built. There was plenty of room for the milk cows and the work horses and the hay loft was full of hay for the winter. The granaries were brimming with corn and rye so the animals would be well fed.

"Wait right here" he said. He opened the door and came back down the steps then proceeded to pick her up and carry her over the threshold.

She squealed "Frank what are you doing?"

"I'm carrying the most beautiful woman in the world into her new home and our new life. I love you Elizabeth and want you to be happy here with me."

"I love you too!" I just hope I can be a good enough wife and partner for such a wonderful man, she thought.

Ed and Earl were waiting for them in the sitting room and she was embarrassed when they saw Frank carrying her in the house. She straightened her coat and dress and said "Hello! Thank you both for taking care of things for us. I've never had a brother so I feel lucky to have three all at once."

They laughed at that and said "do you need help bringing Miss Ro." Ed stopped in mid-sentence "I mean our sister Elizabeth's belongings in to the house?"

"Well, she does have several trunks with her clothes and furnishings, so yes, help would be appreciated." Frank laughed.

"I'm not sure what all we have in the house to eat, but I think I can rustle something up that will at least fill your stomachs." Elizabeth offered.

After the brothers brought her trunks into the house and teased her that everything wouldn't fit in the little house. They ate a light meal and Elizabeth began to unpack and arrange the various gifts and decorations from the wedding. Within a couple of hours, the house was transformed into a home and was cozy and snug.

Ed and Earl planned to go into town to spend the night and said their goodbyes and congratulations to the newlyweds. They would be heading back to California in a couple of days.

As he lit the coal-oil lantern Frank said, "Here we are Mrs. Wagner, just the two of us in our new home. What do you think?"

"I think this is the start of a wonderful life and I'm looking forward to it so much!"

The next morning Elizabeth asked Frank if he would please build a chicken house for her. She felt that if they had chickens, they would always have something to eat and maybe with any luck she could sell the eggs and make a little money. He was surprised by her request and pleased. "Of course! I'll get started as soon as the weather clears up a bit."

"By the way, do you know how to milk a cow?" he asked.

"Um, no, but I'm sure I can learn."

"Good, no time like the present. Come on, put on your coat and hat and some gloves and let's go meet the girls."

The cows were waiting patiently in the barn. They were both Brown Swiss cattle. They were a fawn color with sweet brown eyes and long lashes. Their milk was supposed to be much richer than other breeds, according to Frank. They lowed a little welcome to Frank and readily put their heads into the stanchions to eat the grain he gave them and so they could be milked. Frank got a stool and put a clean bucket under one of the cow's udders.

"This is how you do it" he said as he washed the udder with warm, soapy water he'd brought from the house and proceeded to milk the first cow. Out of nowhere there appeared three cats. "Hello kitties! Ready for some breakfast?" The cats sat in a row and Frank squirted milk into their mouths as they waited patiently.

"Here, Elizabeth, you try."

"Okay, I think I can get the hang of it." She was surprised at how much strength it took to get the milk to flow, but once it started, she was able to milk the other cow without too much trouble. She didn't think she was ready to feed the cats yet so didn't try, that would come later, for now she poured a little milk into an old tin dish.

"Now we have to get this milk to the house and into the cellar to keep it cold. I'm hoping to buy a cream separator this spring so I can sell the cream in town." He was a true entrepreneur, she thought. They'd always be able to get by if they could sell enough eggs and cream.

And so, their daily routine began. Frank did the milking while she made biscuits for breakfast. He had stocked the pantry but she knew she would be responsible for renewing their supplies in the future. Luckily, she knew how to can and preserve food so they wouldn't go hungry – if they had enough money to buy things until a garden could be planted and harvested and they could butcher a steer. Maybe they could buy a couple of pigs too. They had a lot to do in the near future. It was a daunting task, but together they were up for anything.

Elizabeth had never lived so far outside of town before and her new home was very different. In Arkansas their house was on a main road right outside of the city limits and even though they had an acre for a garden, her father was a tailor, not a farmer. Her home in Denver was an apartment above the tailor shop and then she lived with the Schubert's. Farm life was going to take some getting used to. The land stretched flat and barren to the east, as far as she could see. There wasn't another house in sight. There was a knoll on the western edge of their property but other than that the only break in the monotony was sagebrush and an occasional scrub oak tree.

It seemed to her that the wind blew all of the time and no matter how hard she tried, she couldn't keep the dust from accumulating. They did have running water in the house which was fed from the well by a windmill in the corral across the yard. The water was also used for the cattle so if there were cows in the corral or the wind stopped blowing, her water supply was low. Frank had invented an ingenious device to pump the water into the house so she wouldn't have to haul it from the well and she was very happy about that.

The house was furnished with lovely furniture that Frank had made. He was an amazing carpenter and took pride in his work. He shyly showed her a beautiful rocking chair. "For the little ones, when they come along" he said hopefully. She asked if Frank would hang some curtain rods so she could put up the curtains she had made. He thought they really didn't need curtains, living way out in the middle of nowhere, but agreed with a grin. He wanted her to be happy more than anything.

Frank built a solid, handsome chicken house for her and they traded with Elsa Wyman for some laying hens and a young rooster. Elsa wanted one of Frank's wood carvings in exchange. The hens happily settled into their new home and began laying right away.

One morning Elizabeth awoke to the sound of dripping water. The snow on the roof was melting and dripping off the eaves. "Finally, she thought, "spring is here!" She hadn't bargained for all of the mud though. When the snow and ice melted it revealed that there was nothing but dirt around the house and outbuildings. There was a sea of mud everywhere she looked. When she went to the barn or the new chicken house to do chores, she had to be sure her boots didn't get stuck in the mud and come off of her feet. She hoped it would dry out soon, she was already tired of mopping mud off the floor in the house. Try as she might she just couldn't convince Frank that he should take off his muddy boots before he came in. She thought "maybe if he had to clean the floors once in a while, he'd be more willing to keep them from getting so dirty!" But if that was her biggest complaint, she knew it was a minor one.

Saturdays were their day to go to town for supplies and to visit friends. They both looked forward to the trip and were ready to go as soon as the morning chores were done. While Frank went to the hardware store to buy some bolts to repair a broken plow, Elizabeth went to the Schubert's mercantile to shop. Mrs. Schubert had become a good friend and she came around the counter to give Elizabeth a big hug.

"We haven't seen you for ages, Elizabeth" she said. "You look absolutely wonderful. In fact, you're glowing! Do you have a "surprise" for us?"

Elizabeth turned a dark shade of red. "Oh Matilda, I can't believe it's so obvious" she laughed. "Yes, I do have a "surprise" and I need to ask you the name of the doctor who delivered your children." "I haven't even told Frank yet. I hope he'll be as happy as I am."

"Oh my, of course he'll be happy. As a matter of fact, I'll wager he'll be ecstatic! Doc Means delivered all three of my little ones and he's a great doctor, even if he is the only one in the county."

"Thank you. I'll see if I can make an appointment to see him. I'm pretty sure we'll have our "surprise" in about seven months. But I want him to make sure I'm okay. I've had some health issues in the past but I feel as healthy as a horse and have ever since I came to Colorado!" She laughed, "I'm afraid I'm already getting as big as a horse!" She went down the street to Dr. Means' office and asked the receptionist if she could make an appointment to see the doctor.

"Of course!" the receptionist replied, "how about next Saturday at 10:00 a.m. Will that work for you?"

"Yes, that will be fine. I'll see you then." She thought, "Now I just have to break the news to Frank."

Later, on their way home, Elizabeth tucked her hand in the crook of Frank's arm and said, "Do you suppose we could come back into town next Saturday at 10:00 in the morning?"

"Well, I suppose so, why at that particular time though?"

"I have an appointment in town, that's all."

"What kind of appointment?" he asked.

"An appointment with Doc Means."

"Why, are you sick? You haven't mentioned that you weren't feeling well. Are you okay?" he was concerned.

"No, I'm not sick, at least not that kind of sick. But I've been pretty tired lately and my breakfast hasn't been going down all that well."

He looked at her in astonishment. "Are you saying what I think you're saying?"

"Well, if you think I'm saying that we're going to have an addition to the Wagner family, then yes." She laughed out loud at the look on his face.

"Whoa!" He pulled the team over, and turned to her. "Are you sure? How long have you known? Why didn't you tell me? Are feeling okay? I can't believe it! I'm going to be a father!! Thank you! And thank you God, you've answered my prayers." He leaned over and gave her a big hug and kiss. "Now, you have to take it easy. No more milking or working in the garden, or anything strenuous. Oh, I can't believe it! This is wonderful news!"

She laughed "Frank, I'm not an invalid. I'm going to have a baby. It's the most natural thing in the world. And, I'm perfectly capable of doing everything I've been doing for several months at least. I'm glad that you're so happy, I know I am!"

"I love you!"

"And I love you!"

Another chapter in Elizabeth's life was about to begin. That gem was starting to glow brighter and brighter!

## Chapter
# FOUR

Over breakfast Frank said "You know I'll be working the fields now that its Spring, so you'll be alone here most of the time. I'm planning on putting alfalfa in the lower field on the other side of the place and then I'll be working Mrs. Paul's land." He farmed on shares for a widow, Mrs. Paul. He worked her land and she paid him a share of the profit.

"I'll be okay. I've got enough to keep me busy, but I'll miss having you around."

"Oh, I'll be home for dinner and supper every day, don't worry about that!" he laughed.

"Of course, you will, you're a good eater and not too picky, thank goodness!" She didn't think she was the best cook in the county, but Frank appreciated anything she tried, as long as it wasn't too burnt.

"Elizabeth, do you know how to fire a gun?' he asked.

"No! I've never even held one. Why?"

"Well, while I'm not here I want you to be able to defend yourself if you have to. So today we're going to have a lesson in shooting my rifle."

"Okay," she was a little hesitant, but realized that it probably was a good idea. They were isolated and remote.

Frank spent the next hour showing her how to load the rifle and how to handle it safely. They went to the knoll and she practiced shooting at sage brush and the targets Frank had made for her. She was a good aim and Frank felt she'd be okay.

Before he went to harness the horses he said "Don't go out too far by yourself, okay? There are rattle snakes out there, and I know you're a famous snake killer, but rattlers are a lot different than tame old bull snakes. So, don't even think about trying to kill one with a hatchet. There can be coyotes out there too and even though they're more afraid of you than you are of them most of the time, they can be dangerous it they're hungry or sick."

She was surprised that he knew about her adventure with the snake. "Nothing is private in a small town" she thought. Until now she hadn't thought there was anything remotely dangerous in her new world and his warning gave her pause. "Well, I'll just be more aware of things, especially now that I've got another life to protect."

Dr. Means confirmed what she already knew and told them that this little addition would arrive some time in November. They were thrilled and immediately started making plans for the future.

The next Saturday after they ran their errands, they met at the wagon to go home. Frank said, "Look I've got a surprise for you!" He was holding a puppy. It was black and white and was absolutely precious!

"Oh! Where did you get it? It's adorable!"

"***SHE'S*** adorable, it's a girl. I think females make the best pets. Henry Weber's Border collie, Belle, had pups a few weeks ago and he said I could have the pick of the litter. I gave him one of my wood carvings in trade. I figured we could use a dog to help work the cattle and every boy needs a dog, don't you think?"

"Wait a minute, what if it's a girl?"

"Well, since I have three brothers and not one sister, the odds are that we'll have a boy. But whether it's a boy or a girl we need a good dog."

She smiled and took the puppy from him. She snuggled in Elizabeth's arms and licked her chin. "She's perfect! I love her and

I love the fact that I'll have company while you're gone during the day." The puppy sat between them on the wagon seat and slept most of the way home.

"Let's call her Lady, okay? She's such a perfect, little lady."

"Sounds good to me. Lady it is." He scratched the puppy behind her ears and she licked his hand. "I think she likes her new name."

The next weeks were spent training Lady. Frank was patient and consistent and soon she was responding to the basic commands. Next, he began to teach her how to help with the cattle and she picked it up easily. She was a very smart little girl! The addition of the pup changed their days in a delightful way.

"Now I won't worry so much about you here all alone. If anyone comes around, Lady will let you know."

Their lives settled into a nice routine. After eating supper Frank helped her clean up and dried the dishes for her and their evenings were spent preparing for the baby. While Frank built a cradle, Elizabeth knitted booties, bonnets, sweaters and baby blankets. They talked about their future and the plans they had for the farm, buying more cattle next year, and some hogs as well as what they would plant in their garden once Frank got it ready for her. They were both happy and content.

One morning after Frank had gone and she had done her chores, Elizabeth was sitting at her new treadle sewing machine. It was one of her most prized possessions. Her parents had given it to her as a wedding gift knowing that she would put it to good use. She had worked in her father's tailor shop since she was just a child and was able to make beautiful clothes and mend them as well. She had splurged on a bolt of soft flannel at the Schubert's mercantile and was busy making gowns and receiving blankets for the baby. The fabric was pale yellow and so soft she knew the baby would be snug and warm. Suddenly Lady started barking. It wasn't her usual happy bark like when Frank came home, or her playful bark she used when she chased one of the cats. This was a serious almost ferocious bark. Elizabeth got up from the sewing machine and went to the kitchen window. There in the yard in front of the house stood a strange man. He was wearing a calico shirt, leather pants and moccasins, with a blanket around his shoulders for warmth. He was obviously an Indian with shoulder-length gray hair. He was leading a black and white paint pony and they both looked exhausted. She opened the window and called to Lady. "Come here" and let her in the house. "Hello. Can I help you? Do you need something?" She was nervous, but the rifle was sitting beside the kitchen door and she felt she could defend herself if necessary.

He raised his hand to his mouth miming the act of eating and then of drinking. She went to the front porch and called to him. "Wait there, I'll get you something to eat. You can get water from the well and your horse can drink from the water trough in the corral. There's hay in the barn's hay loft. Toss a couple of forkfuls down to him while he's in the corral." Lady whined and stayed by her side.

He understood her and led the horse to the corral and tied him to the hitching rail by the trough, then went into the barn. While he was getting the hay, she found some biscuits, a couple of slices of bacon and some hard-boiled eggs left from breakfast. She had some dried apples in the cellar she could give him. She put the food on a plate and set it outside along with a cup of milk. As the horse ate the hay, the man sat on the step and ate his food. When they were both finished, he got on the horse, nodded to her as she stood in the kitchen window and rode away. She and Lady watched him leave with a relieved sigh.

"That was scary wasn't it? The dog whined a little and put her paw on Elizabeth's knee. "You were so brave! You did your job very well. I know, we probably shouldn't have fed him, but he and the horse looked tired and hungry. Frank will probably scold me for not just ignoring him, but I couldn't turn him away." She went back to her sewing. Her hands were actually trembling a little. "Oh well, 'all's well that ends well'."

When Frank got home that evening, she told him about her strange visitor. "Of course, you did the right thing, but please be careful in the future. Not everyone is friendly or harmless." "You know this used to be a major hunting area for the Indians around here. There were several different tribes that shared this hunting ground. I've been told there were large herds of buffalo and hundreds of antelope. As a matter of fact, I've found several arrow and spear heads when I've been plowing the fields. I've kept them in a wooden box in my bureau."

"I had no idea! What happened to the Indians?" she asked.

"They weren't aggressive and actually helped the settlers when they were headed out west. Between diseases that they had no defense against and the fact that we started farming and fenced their land they were driven out. A lot of them are up in South Dakota and Montana." "This fellow was pretty far away from home, no wonder he looked tired and hungry."

"Now I feel better that I helped him. The poor man, he had a long ride ahead of him. I hope he made it."

The weather had been perfect for farming, not too much rain or wind and just enough sun to make things grow and produce a good crop. The traveling harvesters showed up one sunny August morning with their work horses and machinery and began harvesting Frank's crops. They came through at the same time every year, starting in Texas and moving on up through Kansas, Nebraska, Colorado and on to Canada. They were there just long enough to harvest the wheat and corn for Frank and anyone else who had hired them the year before. Elizabeth's job was to feed them dinner every day which meant making enough for an army of hungry men. She spent her mornings cooking and her afternoons cleaning. It was a sort of competition between the farm wives to see who could make the best dinner for the men. Elizabeth knew she wasn't a great cook but hoped quantity would outweigh quality. As Frank paid them, she was kind of glad to see them move on but knew they'd be back next year bringing their equipment and their appetites with them.

Frank made arrangements with a neighbor who fancied himself as quite a cowboy, to help him round up the steers he was going to sell and take them into town. They would be put into a holding corral near the railroad tracks until the beef buyers came and bought them. Frank's herd was fat and healthy and he knew he would get a good price for them, if the buyers were fair.

The crops and the beef were their livelihood and the prices they got would either make them or break them. Their future depended on the money they made now. Luckily the buyers were generous and offered Frank even more than he had hoped and crop prices were up nicely. Things looked good for the upcoming year. Now they could pay the doctor to deliver the baby, buy that cream separator they had talked about and could buy some hogs too. They had made a deal with a nearby neighbor to bring his bull to their cattle and they hoped there would be a nice crop of baby calves in the spring. Maybe next year they could get their own bull. The future was promising. Elizabeth's garden was productive as well. She had canned and dried enough fruit and vegetables to last them over the winter. It was a good feeling to look at the rows of jars full of fruit and vegetables, along with applesauce and jam on the shelves, and the barrels of potatoes, carrots and apples and strings of onions and garlic hanging from the rafters in the root cellar. They had come a long way in the past year.

It was decided that when Elizabeth's time to deliver the baby neared, her mother would come and stay with them. She would help with things and just give Elizabeth a little extra moral support while she took care of their new baby. Doc Means thought the baby would be born in November around Thanksgiving. Her mother was coming on the train and Frank would meet her and bring her out to the ranch. They spent several days preparing the extra bedroom for her mother to use while she was with them. The baby would move in there when it got old enough. Now, they waited with excitement to meet the newest member of their little family. Elizabeth's mother arrived the week before Thanksgiving and together they would prepare a feast to share with the Schubert's. They were all coming out to the ranch for dinner. This would be the first time she had actually had company for dinner and Elizabeth was nervous. Luckily her mother was there to help.

Thanksgiving morning was cold and hazy, that Autumn haze that makes things look closer than they really are. Elizabeth awoke with a strange feeling. She was full of energy and couldn't lie still. She had a backache and couldn't seem to get comfortable in bed so got up earlier than usual. She stoked the fire in the woodstove and started to make coffee and batter for pancakes. Frank had been doing the milking for the past few weeks when her belly got too big for her to sit easily on the milking stool. She started out to gather some eggs for breakfast but barely got out the door when a whoosh of water ran down her legs, soaking her skirt. "I think my water just broke" she thought. She knew this was a sign that she was in labor. "That's why my back is hurting too." She went back into the house and woke Frank. "I think you may need to get Doc Means."

"What?" he was sound asleep. "What do you mean? Are you sick?" He wasn't awake yet and didn't understand what she was trying to tell him. "Your water – what water?" Is there a leak somewhere?"

"No, Frank I think the baby is coming." She smiled.

"Oh my gosh! He jumped up, stubbed his toe on the bed and started to pull on his pants. "Here, sit down, no lie down, are you okay?" He was moving around the room aimlessly looking for his socks and shirt and trying to get dressed, hopping on one foot and then another while he tried to put on his boots. "Don't move, I'll go get the doctor right away." He started out the door with one boot on and one shirt sleeve hanging while he pulled on his jacket.

"Wait. I don't think you have to rush." "This could take a while, but you probably need to let the Schubert's know we won't be having Thanksgiving dinner here after all." He came back and sat on the bed next to her.

"Are you hungry? Do you want me to make you something to eat?"

"No, I'm really not, I can't even think about eating right now." She winced as a contraction started.

"Oh my gosh, you're in pain! Oh no, I'll get your mother!"

She smiled as he knocked on her mother's door. He was going to be such a good father!

Her mother came in wearing her nightdress, checked Elizabeth's forehead just for something to do and said, "We should be timing those pains. How far apart do you think they are, Bethy?"

"I don't really know, they just started. I had a backache when I woke up and then when I started out to the chicken house my water broke."

"Okay, well, we have to keep watching. Honestly you would be better moving around a bit if you can. That keeps things progressing. If you stay too still sometimes your labor can stop." "So, let's have some breakfast, you should try to eat a little something, you're going to need all your strength for what's to come." "You're going to do fine. You are strong and healthy and this is the most natural thing in the world." "Bethy, I'm so glad we moved out of Arkansas and gave you the chance to live a normal, healthy life."

This was the first time Elizabeth's mother had said anything about leaving Arkansas without getting teary-eyed and the first time she'd called her Bethy in a very long time. She hoped her mother had finally come to grips with their family's decision and she didn't blame her any more for their move.

Now, she got up and went into the kitchen. She felt fine for the most part and just wanted to get this over with. After breakfast, Frank hooked the horses up to the wagon and started into town. First to give the Schubert's the news and then to get the doctor. The trip would take several hours and he wanted to get going as soon as possible.

Elizabeth and her mother cleaned the kitchen, washed the dishes and then waited in the sitting room, talking and sharing memories. They timed her contractions using Frank's pocket watch and between pains she started getting things ready for the baby. Her mother put a pan of water on to boil and got some rags and towels ready and they waited. Her mother held her hand to reassure and comfort her. The pains were coming every three minutes when they heard Lady bark her "happy" bark which meant Frank was back. He came in, kissed her cheek, knelt in front of her and asked how she was doing. He told them the doctor was right behind him. She was very happy to see her husband and even happier to know that Doc Means was there too. She knew it was getting close.

The doctor walked in, bringing an air of competence and experience with him, he said "Hello Elizabeth, how're you doing?" and took her pulse.

"Fine! I'm just very glad to see you!"

"Okay, then let's get you into your bed and take a look." "Your breathing and pulse are strong and regular. You're going to be just fine. Well, it looks like my timing was impeccable again. I'm pretty good at gauging these things you know" he said with a laugh.

"Mrs. Ross, is it, you're Elizabeth's mother? Please bring me that water you've got heated and some towels and Frank will you please light the coal oil lantern? We've got a baby to deliver."

Soon, the pains were strong and regular. She was glad to realize that this was something she could tolerate. Then she felt an urge to push and before too long she heard a little whimper then a full-fledged cry. Doc Means held up a little pink wriggling being by it's feet and said, you folks have yourselves a nice, healthy baby boy!" "Here Mrs. Ross, take him and clean him up a little so your daughter can hold her new son." "Frank, can you fetch the scale out of my buggy so we can see just how big this little man is?"

Later Frank held Elizabeth's hand and smoothed her hair off her forehead. He said, "You were so brave Thank you for my son, I love you both!" She smiled and touched his cheek. "OUR son, we have a son!"

The baby weighed seven pounds seven ounces and was twenty-one inches long, according to the doctor, a perfect size for a first baby. He packed his implements into his bag and prepared to leave. "I'll file the birth certificate tomorrow. What is his name?"

Elizabeth looked up at Frank, he nodded and she said "we want to name him Charles Franklin Wagner, after my father and his own father" Elizabeth said. Frank smiled proudly.

"Good strong name. Congratulations and Happy Thanksgiving! You truly have something to be thankful for."

Elizabeth's mother cleaned the baby, dressed him in one of the gowns Elizabeth had made, and gave him to her wrapped snugly in his new blanket. There were tears of joy in her mother's eyes as she watched her daughter kiss her new son.

Frank sat beside her as she nursed the baby. He was perfect, with blond hair like his father, and a little turned-up nose like his mother. "This is truly a miracle. God is good!"

Elizabeth's mother went home after a few days. She hated to see her leave but knew her father and sister needed her at home. As she sat in the rocking chair and looked at her new son, she felt a tremendous surge of love. The next chapter in Elizabeth's life began. The gem was brighter than ever.

## Chapter
# FIVE

Charles was a good baby, Elizabeth felt he was good because she and Frank were so happy to be parents and they were both calm and mellow natured people. He grew steadily and by Christmas he was holding his head up and looking around like a little old man. His eyes would latch onto something bright and stare interestedly until something else caught his attention. Frank spent his spare time making a set of building blocks for Charles for Christmas.

"I'm pretty sure he won't know what to do with those blocks for quite a while" she laughed. "He'll most likely try to eat them first."

They were solid and colorful and perfectly smooth so no splinters would get into tiny fingers or tongues!

"I couldn't decide whether to make blocks or a rocking horse, so I opted for the blocks this year. The horse will be for next Christmas" he said. "By then he should be able to sit on it and make it rock. It'll get him ready for a real pony, maybe when he's two."

"Can you make him a rattle or something he can teethe on?" she asked. "I'm going to make him a mobile out of paper snowflakes to hang over his cradle. It should keep his interest and help him learn to focus his little eyes."

"Okay, I'll try to make some little balls and string them on a piece of rawhide. He can chew on the balls and the string. That'll keep him busy after he chews up the paper snowflakes" he teased.

"Oh, I never thought of that! He just *might* chew them and maybe even choke on them!"

"I was just kidding Elizabeth! He won't be able to reach anything that's hanging from his cradle for several months and by then we'll give him something else to play with."

"Oh look, he's smiling! Maybe it's gas? Isn't he amazing – all the faces he makes seem like he's trying to tell us something. He'll probably be talking before we know it!"

"He's going to be really smart just like his Mama."

"And tall and handsome just like his Daddy."

They were over the moon in love with their son.

Lady started barking. It wasn't her happy or playful bark. She was barking a warning.

Frank looked out the kitchen window "Looks like we've got company. I thought the Schubert's were coming for dinner tomorrow for Christmas." No, wait it's just one rider and he's leading a little foal."

Elizabeth joined him at the window and gasped "Frank, it's that Indian fellow that was here a few months ago. I wonder where he's going this time."

Frank went to the front door with Elizabeth following close behind. She made sure the rifle was in its spot by the door. "Hello!" Frank called. "Can we help you?" The Indian stopped in the yard in front of the house again and held his hand up with the palm facing Frank as though to say "Stop" but in reality, he was saying "hello". He waved for Frank to come out. Frank called to Lady, stepped off the porch and approached the man with his hand outstretched and he shook it in a gesture of friendship.

Elizabeth thought, "What a lovely little filly!" She was a black and white paint, just like the horse the man was riding. Her mane had been combed and bells were braided into it. They jingled when she shook her head and she seemed to like to hear them ring.

As Frank neared the man, he looked up and gestured for Elizabeth to come closer too. She stepped off the porch and went to stand beside Frank. When she reached the two men the Indian handed her the end of the lead-rope he was holding. He was giving the filly to her.

"Oh, my no! I don't know what to say… What should I do Frank?!?"

The man spoke in halting English. "You fed, this is thank you." So tired, couldn't go any more. Food helped make home. Please take. Good horse, good home."

She was overwhelmed with this generous gesture. "I'm so glad that you made it safely. We've spoken of you many times and wondered how you fared. This gift is more than I deserve, but I will, *WE* will, love her and take good care of her. You can come visit her any time. You are welcome here. Thank you."

The man mounted his horse and turned to leave. Frank called "Would you like some food for your journey?"

The man reached into his saddle bag and took out a package wrapped in buckskin. He leaned down from his horse, handed it to Elizabeth and said "for baby". He pointed to his other saddle bag and said "Got food, is OK" and he rode away.

Elizabeth and Frank looked at each other in disbelief. "I guess everyone knows about the Golden Rule" she said as she unwrapped the package. It was a dried gourd with seeds inside – a rattle for the baby. The stem was wrapped in leather for a handle and a lovely scrolled design was made on the gourd with a sharp instrument of some kind. "Charles will love this, don't you think?" Frank nodded his head in wonder.

He took the hand-braided lead rope and led the filly to the barn. She tried to follow the other horse as the man left, but didn't seem too upset when she couldn't go with them. Frank put her in the barn with the work horses and gave them all some grain. She settled right in as though she'd been there forever. The big horses were curious, especially about the bells in her mane, but were careful not to step on her. They seemed to realize she was just a baby.

"I wonder where that man lives?" Elizabeth asked.

"He looks like he's Sioux. He's probably from the Ogallala Sioux tribe near Ogallala, Nebraska. They've had a long ride."

Elizabeth looked at the pretty little filly. "It's your turn, what do you want to call her?"

"She's your gift, so you have to name her, its tradition."

"Are you sure? OK, let's see, how about Sue since she's from the Sioux tribe. Do you like that?"

"Well, she does look like an Indian pony doesn't she? Come here Sue." The little horse stopped eating and looked up at him. "Yep, she seems to like that name. It's easy to say and that'll help when I'm training her."

Is that the baby I hear? I'd better go see if he's okay. Goodbye Sue. I'll see you in a bit." And she hurried off to the house.

Frank scratched his head "Who would have imagined? My wife is quite a woman."

## Chapter
# SIX

The next year went by quickly and peacefully. Their cattle herd was growing and her chickens were multiplying nicely. But, the spring when Charlie was a year and a half old the weather changed. There was no rain for weeks and then there would be a downpour, washing the seeds away before they could take hold and germinate. Frank watched the sky anxiously every morning, hoping for a good, soaking rain, but the rain clouds were few and far between and the wind seemed to blow the topsoil all the way to Kansas. The corn finally started to grow and they were both hopeful that they would have some sort of crop after all.

One afternoon, black storm clouds built up in the west. Elizabeth watched from the front porch as the storm neared. She hurried to the corral and put Sue in the barn. The milk cows were in the near pasture and she sent Lady to bring them in. She was such a good dog and Frank had trained her well. The clouds were moving fast and she had barely gotten the cows in, and the barn closed when the rain started. She and Lady ran to the house and slammed the door just as it started to pour, then as she watched, the rain turned to hail. The hailstones were small to start with but got bigger and bigger as the storm increased. She stood in the kitchen and watched the hail completely demolish her garden. All of her carefully tended vegetables were shredded to bits. There was nothing left except the ripped ribbons of leaves. She wanted to cry.

Suddenly there was a change in the wind and the sky darkened even more. The clouds were black and ominous and seemed to nearly touch the top of the bluff west of their house. As she watched she saw a tail come down out of the clouds and twist around heading toward the ground. It was a funnel cloud. She ran into the bedroom and grabbed the sleeping Charlie out of his bed and headed for the root cellar. She had trouble opening the door, the wind kept blowing it out of her hands and she had even more trouble opening the heavy cellar door. Charlie clung to her like a monkey, crying in fear. After what seemed like forever, she got the cellar door open enough for her to carry the baby and get Lady down the steps. She pulled the door closed and locked it behind them, lit the coal oil lantern and sat on a stool in the far corner away from the door. She held Charlie on her lap and soothed him until he stopped crying and then waited for the storm to pass over.

She was frantic for Frank. He was working in Mrs. Paul's field about 3 miles to the northeast – the path the storm appeared to be taking. She knew there was no shelter there and he and his team were at the mercy of this horrible storm. She prayed he had seen it coming and had at least gotten under a wagon or something.

As she sat in the cellar, she heard what sounded like a freight train roar over their little house. The cellar door banged and rattled, but held tight. Charlie started crying again and she clutched him closer to her chest. Lady sat at her knee whining. Then just as soon as the storm started it stopped and everything was quiet. Too quiet, she thought. She didn't know whether she was in the eye of the storm or if it had passed over them. "Do tornadoes have eyes?" she wondered. "Or is that hurricanes" She was shaking all over. She waited for several minutes and finally decided to venture out to see if everything was alright.

She put Charlie on the floor in the corner and told him to wait there for her, just in case the storm wasn't really over, and carefully opened the cellar door. The sky was a pale-yellow color, like nothing she had ever seen. The air felt sharp and smelled acrid. She looked around. There didn't seem to be too much damage. Some of the trees Frank had planted were uprooted, and one had blown into a grain silo. The chicken house was on its side but was in one piece. She could hear the chickens carrying on inside. The barn itself seemed to be okay, but part of the roof had blown away. One wall of the house was missing in the sitting room and several of the windows were broken, but the roof was intact.

She got Charlie and went to the barn to check on the livestock. Sue was shivering in the corner and the milk cows were leaning on each other as though to give each other comfort. They greeted her when she opened the door. They were okay, but she knew rain would drench the hay if they didn't get the roof fixed.

Her first thought was for her husband. "Please God, don't let anything have happened to Frank." She had never felt so helpless in her life. Should she try to saddle Sue and ride to where he was working or walk? She was afraid the filly wasn't well-trained or big enough to carry her and Charlie safely. Ultimately, she decided to walk. It was only two or three miles. She should be able to walk that easily. It had gotten hot, really hot. The clouds had passed over but the sky was still that sickly yellow color and the stillness was stifling. She made a sling out of her shawl, put Charlie on her back and started walking down their lane with Lady at her side.

As she walked, she kept repeating "Please be okay, please be okay, please be okay." She had walked for about a mile when she saw something in the distance. It was a man on horseback. "Oh, please let it be Frank" she thought. Yes, it was Frank. He was riding one of the work horses, and the other was following behind, but limping badly. Frank had a gouge on his forehead and blood was dripping onto his shirt. He was holding his left arm awkwardly against his side. It looked like it was broken. She started to run toward him and he urged the horses to go faster too. When they reached each other he dismounted and ran to her. "Oh my God! I am so happy to see you! Are you alright?" They both said in unison. They held onto each other, as though afraid to let go. The little family stood together in a cluster, thanking God that they were safe.

Finally, she said "We're fine. Charlie, Lady and I made it to the root cellar just in time. But what happened to you?"

"I'm okay too. I heard the wind coming and tried to get the horses to a safe spot in a little gully. We almost made it but things were flying around and I got hit in the head by a piece of wood and a fence post came flying through the air and hit my arm and Nick's hip. I'm afraid my arm might be broken and I hope Nick doesn't have a broken leg. We need to have a look at it when we get to the barn. Is everything okay at home?"

"There was some damage, but nothing too bad. Part of the roof on the barn got blown away and one wall is gone in the house. I hope you can help me put the chicken house back up, it's laying on its side. Other than that, I think we made it through this alright. Oh, except my garden is ruined. The hail got everything."

"Hail? I didn't see any hail. I guess it missed me this time. I think I'd better get to the house and have you look at my arm. It hurts like the dickens."

They put Charlie on Jack's back and Elizabeth led the horses back to the house. Nick was limping badly but Jack seemed okay, he had a couple of cuts and scrapes but nothing serious. When they got to the house, they put the horses in the barn and went into the kitchen. She helped Frank remove his shirt and looked at his arm. It was bent at a weird angle and she agreed with him that it looked broken. Luckily, she didn't see anything protruding through the skin. It seemed like a clean fracture that she could fix with a makeshift splint. She got some thin pieces of wood from Frank's woodshop, put them around his arm and wrapped bandages around it to immobilize it.

"This will do until we can get you to town to see Doc Means. We should go as soon as possible."

"I can't go until I've checked on Nick. I'm really worried about him."

Charlie was exhausted and had fallen asleep. She laid him in his bed and they walked out to the barn together. On the way she asked if he could steady a side of the chicken house while she pushed it over. Together they got it righted and were able to open the door to let the poor chickens out. They had gone in to their nests as soon as the wind and rain had started and were all fine. They were glad to be let out and ran around the yard cackling and pecking the dirt. The rooster was busy making sure his harem was okay. Elizabeth straightened the nests and removed any eggs that had broken.

When they got to the barn, they found Nick standing with one hind foot off the ground. Frank said, "Elizabeth can you take a look at his leg?"

She knelt down beside the gentle giant and checked his hoof, then examined his leg from his ankle to his hip. "You know, I don't feel anything broken. I see a big cut on his flank and I think that's what's bothering him. He doesn't want me to touch it. It's been bleeding but seems to have stopped and it looks pretty clean. I think I can stitch him up and if we put some ointment on it, he'll be okay."

"That's good" Frank breathed a sigh of relief. "Can you get your sewing kit? I'll hold him while you clean the wound and stitch him. Just act like you're mending a pair of my pants."

Elizabeth went to the house to get her sewing kit and checked on Charlie. She then went back to the barn and began to work on Nick's cut. "Okay I think that'll do" she said after a few minutes. "I'll disinfect it and put some salve on it to help it heal and I think he'll be as good as new. Let's get you back into the house."

As they drove to town first thing the next morning, they saw that the hail storm had ruined several crops. It was so strange. The hail would completely raze one field, jump over another one and ruin the next. There was no rhyme or reason to it. When they got to town, they found that the tornado had missed most of the buildings, there wasn't much damage and there were no serious injuries. Doc

Means was able to put a plaster cast on Frank's arm. He said the splint had kept the arm immobilized and enabled him to set the break successfully.

When Wilbur Schubert found out about Frank's arm and the damage to their house and barn, he got several of the men in town to go out to their place with him to repair things. Luckily the group of men was able to fix the wall in the sitting room using materials that were left when Frank built the house and got the barn roof patched by the following day. The windows would have to be ordered from Denver.

Doc Means told Frank that this was a bad break and he would be out of commission for several weeks until the bone in his arm healed. When this news got around several of Elizabeth's older students came to their farm and finished planting the corn on Mrs. Paul's and replanted the wheat and alfalfa crops that Frank had lost in the storm. The people in Hartford and the surrounding area all rallied around each other in times of need.

Elizabeth hoped their luck would change for the better. Things looked pretty grim at the moment, but the fact that they had all survived and had such good friends made her thankful and optimistic about their future.

## Chapter
# SEVEN

The next few weeks were a trial for Elizabeth and Frank. This was the first time they had experienced any real difficulties in their relationship. Frank struggled with his convalescence. He was so accustomed to working with his hands even in the evenings that his inability to even be able to do his wood carvings was horrible for him. He found that a little sip of whiskey helped with the pain in his arm and helped him to relax a little. A little sip turned into a few more and he found himself looking forward to the numbing affects – not only to his arm but to his mind as well. There were several nights that he "fell asleep" in his chair after dinner and Elizabeth couldn't rouse him to come to bed. Lately, he'd started drinking first thing in the morning and spent most of his day sitting in his chair drinking and feeling sorry for himself.

Elizabeth was worried. She wondered if she'd been hasty in marrying Frank. After all she really didn't know that much about him, just what the Schubert's had told her. This new side of him was not pleasant. He was short with her and especially with Charles. The baby's crying bothered him no end and he'd even gotten to the point that any noise at all from the child was unacceptable. Of course, Charlie didn't understand what was happening and eventually started to avoid Frank completely. Their little happy family seemed to be a thing of the past.

After several weeks it was time for Frank to visit Doc Means. The doctor greeted Frank and Elizabeth in the waiting room and escorted Frank back to the examination room. He noticed that Charles seemed quiet and subdued. Elizabeth's face was wan, she looked haggard and exhausted.

"Well Frank it looks like your arm is healing nicely." Doc Means said as he removed the cast and began to replace it with a smaller one. "How's everything else? Are you eating and sleeping well?"

"I'm doing as well as can be expected, Doc. After all, I'm pretty much an invalid. You know I can't even milk a cow and can barely lift a forkful of hay for the livestock. I'll be awfully glad to be back to normal. Watching everything go to hell is tough."

"Yes, I imagine this is difficult for you. How's Elizabeth doing? Is Charlie okay?"

"She's doing okay, I guess. Everything has fallen on her shoulders. I'm thinking of asking one of my brothers to come back for a few weeks to help in the fields. As for Charlie, he doesn't want to spend much time with me any more. I guess since I can't play ball or give him piggy back rides he doesn't have much use for me either."

"Frank, this may not be any of my business, but I smell alcohol on your breath. Are you drinking?"

"You're right Doc, this isn't any of your business. I take a little sip of whiskey now and then to help with the pain. It's just for medicinal purposes, nothing permanent, just to get me through this rough patch."

"I think you're doing more than taking a little sip now and then, Frank. I've always liked and respected you. You have a nice family and I hate to think you might be doing something to jeopardize it. If there's anything I can do to help you get through this "rough patch" as you call it, please let me know. It's not fair to your wife and son. Just give this some thought and come back in three weeks so I can take this cast off."

Elizabeth and Charlie were quiet on the ride home. Frank couldn't stop thinking about what the doctor said. However, he had a stubborn streak and he didn't think that he'd changed that much. After all, this was a hard thing for a man to cope with, and he was doing the best he could. Or so he thought.

Elizabeth was exhausted with the effort of trying to cope with everything that was going on, but one thing was for sure she wasn't a quitter. She just had to think of something that would distract Frank and give him a challenge that was doable and hopefully the man she married would resurface. This was their life and the future was good if they could pull together as a team.

One morning she heard Charlie in his room. The little boy was galloping around his room riding the stick horse Frank had made him. She thought, "I wonder if Sue is big enough to start learning some manners." This just might be the answer to their problem. It would give her husband something to do that he could accomplish with just one hand and her son could be with him and learn how to ride a real horse. Sue was a good little girl and she would be able to carry the toddler without any trouble while Frank led her around the paddock.

When she approached Frank with her idea, he was reluctant at first but after a few minutes of considering what she was proposing he said, "You know I think you're right. I think I can work with the filly and she sure could use some training. I'll get her started this morning after breakfast. Do you think Charlie would like to help?"

With a sigh of relief, she replied "Oh Frank, I think he'd love to help. He rides his stick horse all of the time and I think he's big enough to sit on Sue's back while you lead her around. This could be a good thing for all of you!"

So, the training began. At first Elizabeth had to help Frank with the halter but after the filly got used to it, she was happy to follow Frank around while he talked soothingly to her and got her to do what he was asking. Elizabeth noticed that Frank hadn't bothered to take a drink that morning. Maybe he just needed something to do. After a few days it was time for Charlie to sit on the filly's back. He was ecstatic! He'd wanted to ride a real horse and now here he was, sitting up high on her back with her mane in his little hands. Together they worked on Sue and Charlie's training, and Frank was content to spend his days working with his son and the horse. Things were looking up.

Soon it was time for Frank to go back in to see Doc Means and have the cast removed for good. They were a much different group on this trip than the last one. They were talking and laughing and were so much happier than they had been just a few weeks ago.

When Doc Means called Frank into his office, he noticed the marked change in the entire family and was glad to see that Frank didn't smell of whiskey this time. He said to Frank, "I'm very happy to see how you're recuperating, Frank. This has been a difficult situation for you and your family, but it looks like you've all come through it in good shape."

"Thanks Doc, you were right and I appreciate the fact that you said something to me. I just needed a healthy kick in the rear end and a wife who didn't give up on me. Things should improve from here on out."

Frank was apologetic and promised that he would not let this happen again. Elizabeth was happy that things were getting back to normal, but she wouldn't forget this set-back and would be wary for a while. "Experience is the best teacher", she thought.

## Chapter

# *EIGHT*

A few weeks later Elizabeth worked in her newly planted garden while Charlie dug in the dirt nearby. Lady gave her "somebody's coming" bark and Elizabeth watched as a lone rider appeared at the end of their road. She picked Charlie up and they went into the house. As the rider neared, she recognized the boy that worked in the Western Union office in town. A chill went down her spine. "This can't be good news" she thought. Telegrams rarely bring joy and this was no exception. She met the young man in the yard and read the telegram. The wire was from her father; it said that her mother was very ill and asked Elizabeth to come to Denver, right away. She gave the messenger a light snack and he went on his way with a reply telling her father that she would be there as soon as possible. She began to pack a suitcase for herself and Charlie. She knew that her mother had been ill but didn't know how serious it was. Her mind was racing and her hands shook as she made a list of things to take and a list of the chores Frank would have to do while she was gone.

When Frank came in from the field for dinner, she met him with the news. He said "We need to get you into town as soon as possible so you can catch the next train to Denver. Don't worry everything here will be okay, just tell your mother I'm praying for her and your father and sister, and of course I'll pray for you."

They spent the rest of the day getting things in order for her trip. After a sleepless night they left first thing the next morning. The train left at 9:00 a.m., she and Charlie were at the station at 8 and were one of the first people on board. As the train left the station, she and her son waved out the window at Frank. He looked forlorn standing there all alone and she worried that he might have a relapse. She shook herself, no time for unnecessary worry she had to get through the next few days.

Her father was at the train station in Denver when she arrived. His face was drawn and he'd obviously not slept for days. Her sister Lois was at home with their mother. This wasn't a good sign. They collected her luggage and immediately went to her parents' house.

Elizabeth was shocked at how pale her mother was. Her face was almost as white as the pillow case and her hair was completely white. She looked as though she was in terrible pain. When she heard Elizabeth enter the room, she opened her eyes and held out her hand to her daughter and her grandson. "Bethy, I've been waiting for you. Oh my, is this little Charlie? He's a fine, big boy isn't he?" Talking seemed to wear her out. She was so weak that all she could do was to lay her head back down and close her eyes.

"Momma, is there anything I can do for you? Do you want some water or tea? Are you hungry?" Elizabeth felt so helpless but she was glad that she had gotten there in time to be with her mother. It was obvious that she wasn't going to live much longer. She tried to hide her tears but they were streaming down her cheeks. Lois was sitting next to their mother, holding her hand. She'd been reading the bible to her mother just for something to do – for both of them.

"I'm so glad you're here Beth. I'm really scared but I know that Momma is in so much pain that it's not fair to want her to live like this. Sarah is expecting another baby and is due any day so she couldn't' travel. She's beside herself that she can't be here with Momma." The sisters were sitting in the kitchen while their mother's doctor checked on her. Their father was with the doctor in her room.

Charlie was quiet, his eyes were troubled and he was having a hard time understanding what was wrong with his Granny.

When the doctor came downstairs, he asked Elizabeth and Lois to join him in the parlor. "I'm sure you realize that your mother is dying. I know this is hard to hear, but she has been hanging on until you and your son arrived. As you know, she has cancer and by the time she came to me it was too late. She's a brave woman and I'm sure she has been a wonderful wife and mother. I wish I had known her when she was healthy. Even in the midst of her illness she is a delightful person."

"Yes, she is. We will all miss her terribly but we can't stand to see her suffer. Is there anything you can do to ease her pain?'

"I'm doing everything I can to make her comfortable but it won't be long now I'm sorry to say."

"Thank you, Doctor. Will you be back later today?"

"Yes, I'll check on her before I go home for the day. Just spend time with her and cherish your last few hours with her."

After the doctor left, Elizabeth took a tray upstairs to her mother. She wasn't able to eat anything of course but she was happy to see Elizabeth. "Bethy, could you lie down here with me? I'm so cold and it would be nice if you would hold me."

"Of course, Momma, do you want another blanket? Daddy and Lois are making dinner. Charlie is always hungry these days. Is there anything you want or need?'

"Not really, I just need to rest. Every little thing seems to tire me out."

Elizabeth laid down beside her mother and held her close. Her body was so frail, Elizabeth was afraid she might hurt her. After a while her mother said "Beth, call your father and sister. I need them to come up here now."

"Oh Momma. I'll call them right now."

"Daddy, Lois, come up here right away! Momma needs you both!"

Surrounded by her loving family, Elizabeth's mother quietly

left this earth. She left a huge void in the family and they would all grieve for her for the rest of their lives. The doctor returned shortly after her mother passed away and prepared the necessary legal documents.

During the next few days the funeral arrangements were made and the grief-stricken little family bid their beloved mother farewell. Elizabeth and Charlie made the long, sad trip back to their home in Hartford.

## Chapter

# NINE

Frank was eagerly waiting for his family to return. He had been lonely while they were gone. He missed the everyday noises and activities, the singing and laughter, the rattle of pots and the clatter of little feet. He had gotten accustomed to having Elizabeth and then Charlie in his life and now that they were away the void was tangible.

As he sat in his empty house, he remembered the time when he lived alone on the ranch and how he'd had to manage on his own. One particularly bad spring snow storm came to mind and how his underlying faith had been restored. As a farmer he always felt close to nature and believed in the existence of a higher power. He was aware of how dependent and vulnerable he was. He always thought of it as "The Blizzard". It was the spring before he married Elizabeth. A storm had come up without any warning. When he looked out the kitchen window everything was white and covered with snow. The wind was howling, blowing the falling snow into drifts against anything that was stationary. The drifts had been accumulating over several days and in some places they were over 8 feet tall. He had shoveled a path from the house to the wood pile and another from the house to the barn. But it was a constant chore to keep them clear. The livestock were safely closed into the barn just before the storm hit. He had to venture out into the storm twice each day to feed the animals and to take them fresh water. He was alone on the farm.

At 21 he had found this piece of land and had staked a claim to it. He had improved the land and fenced a portion of it with the help of his brothers. They weren't interested in farming but were willing to help him get settled. He had worked hard - dug a well, built a big barn and corrals, and planted crops. It had taken him several years, but he was proud of his place and wanted to share it with a family. He'd spent the last year building a new house for his soon-to-be wife. The wood stove used for heating and cooking kept the little house warm and snug. He didn't get lonely then; he was used to being alone. Farming was a solitary occupation and it gave him time to plan for the future and to reflect on the past. He was going to marry Elizabeth at Christmas later that year. He hoped that he would be able to support a wife and family and felt that she would be a good partner.

He pulled on his boots, put on his hat and coat and started out to the barn. When he opened the door, he saw that there was a foot high snowdrift against the threshold. The force of the wind hit him in the face and pushed him back inside, the door flew out of his hands. He had to use both hands to push the door closed and left a pile of snow on the kitchen floor. Trying once again, he was able to get outside and close the door behind him. He found himself in the middle of a freezing whirlwind of blowing snow. He stopped at the well and filled the buckets with water for the livestock. Where was the path he'd cleared? He started walking in the direction of the barn and began counting his steps. He had heard of people becoming disoriented in these white-out conditions and getting lost. Even though he knew his farm like the back of his hand. he'd measured his steps carefully and knew that it was exactly two hundred and thirteen paces from the door to the barn.

It took him quite a while to get there but he made it safely. The horses and cattle greeted him and ate and drank gratefully. He sat with them for a while, just to feel their warmth and share their company. Being there with them was comforting. It was getting dark and once again he struggled against the wind trying to follow his own footsteps back to the house. They were already full of snow and hard to see. He counted his steps and when he reached two hundred thirteen, he should have been at the door, but there was nothing. Where did he go wrong? Had he veered to the left or right without knowing it? He turned around and started back to the barn. It was darker now and he had trouble seeing the foot prints he'd just made in the snow. He should have brought a lantern, but hadn't expected to be out in the dark and his hands were full with the water buckets. He took two hundred and thirteen steps but the barn wasn't there. Now what? It was getting colder and darker by the minute and the wind and snow continued to blow. There was no one to hear him if he called out – he was totally alone. Completely disoriented now, he stopped and stood still for just a few minutes. Which way should he go? He wasn't particularly religious, he didn't go to church, but he prayed, "God please don't let me freeze to death. The animals will starve or die of thirst." At that moment, the wind died down and he was able to get his bearings. He looked to his left and saw a light in the dark. He headed toward the light. As he got nearer, he saw a lantern shining in the window of his house. He didn't remember leaving a light burning. That would have been wasteful. He pushed hard against the door and with a sigh of relief he practically fell into the warmth of his kitchen expecting it to be filled with light. But it was completely dark. How could this be? The light from the kitchen had led him home. Someone must have been watching over him and heard him after all. He got down on his knees and thanked God for helping him find his way – back home and back to Him.

"Whew!" he thought, "what brought that old memory back?" He shook himself and stood up. Whenever he remembered The Blizzard, he said a silent prayer of thanks. He hoped Elizabeth and Charlie would be home soon; he needed the reassurance of their presence. "Come on Lady, let's go feed the animals." At least he had the little dog for company.

# *TEN*

A couple of days later when he came in from the field he found an envelope tacked to the door. It was a telegram from Elizabeth. This time it was good news – she and Charlie were coming home. It was Wednesday and they would be home on Saturday. His heart filled with joy – until he opened the door and saw what a mess the house was in. He started cleaning the little house. He heated water and washed his dishes, swept the floors and changed the sheets on the bed. There was dust everywhere – of course it was always dusty. The wind blew all the time and there was nothing but dirt around the farm house. He was ashamed of how much mud he'd tracked in – no wonder Elizabeth complained and reminded him to take off his boots when he came in. He dusted the furniture, scrubbed the floors and made a mental note to be better about helping to keep the place clean.

He cleaned up the wood shavings he'd dropped while he made a train set for Charlie. He'd spent his evenings making the locomotive – the wheels turned smoothly and the doors to the cab opened and closed. It was a pretty piece even if he did think so himself. He wanted to surprise his son and give it to him for Christmas. He smiled to himself. As he pictured Charlie playing on the floor – pushing the locomotive around as it pulled the train cars behind it.

Saturday morning was warm and clear and he was up before dawn, doing the chores, anxious to see his wife and son. He got to town before the train arrived and was able to go to Schubert's store to get a bag of licorice for Charlie and a spool of ribbon for Elizabeth. He'd brought Lady along. She'd whined when he tried to leave so he put her in the wagon. She sat on the seat next to him and watched the world go by.

The train was right on time as he waited on the platform, impatient to get the first glimpse of his family. There they were! Charlie bounded down the steps and ran to him "Daddy!! I'm home! I rode on a train and it was big and made a lot of noise and smoke came out of the chimney! Lady! Momma, Lady's here too!" Frank picked the child up and swung him in the air. The little boy couldn't contain his excitement and Frank and Lady were just as happy to see him!

Elizabeth came down the steps next. Frank was at the bottom to help her off the train and to carry her suitcase. "Oh Frank, we've missed you so much! It's so good to be home." She looked at Franks face, saw that his eyes were clear and she breathed a sigh of relief. He was his old self, no hint of alcohol on his breath. She'd worried that he might slip while she was away, but he looked wonderful!

She stood on her tiptoes and gave him a kiss. "I have so much to tell you, but first can we stop at Schubert's? I need to order some fabric for Lois's wedding dress. I know it's expensive, but now that Mother is gone it's up to me to do this. I hope you don't mind."

"What? Lois's getting married? When? Of course, I don't mind. We got a pretty good crop after all the help from our friends and neighbors. We'll be okay."

"Oh, they won't be married for a while. I'll tell you all about it on the trip home. I'm so glad to be going back to the farm."

After ordering the fabric and picking up some other supplies the little family loaded their belongings into the wagon. Frank whistled to Nick and Jack, lifted the reins and they were on their way home. Charlie and Lady sat in the back on a blanket and soon they were both sound asleep.

"So, tell me how's everything at home? You look thin – did you eat while I was gone? Are the chickens laying? How's Sue? Just listen to me, going on and on. I'm just so happy to be home and to see you! I missed you so much!"

"Well, everything's fine at home. Yes, the chickens are still laying – but not as much. Sue's doing great! She's a pleasure to work with, she's so smart and picks things up real fast. I've been eating, but I ran out of the good stuff pretty soon after you left. I forgot how bad of a cook I am." He grinned down at her. "I'll be happy to have a good meal again. I'm glad you're home too. I missed you both, more than you know. Oh, the harvesters will be here next week."

"The harvesters are coming? I hope I have enough food put by to feed them." Actually, she was happy that they were coming. She wouldn't have time to feel sad and grieve for her mother. She had a lot to do when she got home. Her garden had come back fairly well after the tornado and hail storm and she had a lot of canning and drying to do. This time of year was a very busy one. She settled next to Frank and put her head on his shoulder.

"Tell me about Lois. You said she's getting married?"

"Oh yes. She met a very nice young man a few months ago and they've been planning to get married for a while. My father likes him and Lois is all starry-eyed. His name is Jacob and he seems to have a good head on his shoulders. He's a mechanic. You know there are all kinds of motor cars all over Denver and he's got a good business keeping them repaired and on the roads. Of course, they won't get married for a while. We're all still mourning, but we can start making plans."

She felt such happiness in her heart when they came in sight of the farm. This was where she belonged. She couldn't wait to get back into the daily routine of her life.

## Chapter
# *ELEVEN*

The days flew by and before she knew it, it was Thanksgiving and Charlie's second birthday was just days away. The Schubert's were coming for dinner again this year and for once Elizabeth didn't feel overwhelmed. She'd finally figured out how to put a true meal together and get everything done and on the table at the same time.

They truly had a lot to be thankful for this year. Christmas was just around the corner and they were all looking forward to it. Charlie didn't really understand what the excitement was all about but ran around singing "shingle bells, shingle bells" while everyone clapped and laughed. He had no idea who Santa Claus was but the Schubert kids were happy to tell him all about the fat little elf that would bring him a toy and maybe even an orange.

Frank couldn't wait for the holiday to arrive. He had made the passenger car and the caboose for Charlie's train and just had to put the finishing touches on them and paint them. They were so pretty. He knew the little boy would love his train set. He had a surprise for Elizabeth as well. He'd found a lovely cameo brooch at Schubert's store and had asked Mrs. Schubert to put it on hold while he made weekly payments on it. He kept a little back each week when they sold eggs and cream in town to pay for the pin. He hoped Elizabeth would like it. In spite of the problems they'd had earlier in the year, things were settling down.

A couple of weeks after Thanksgiving Frank and Elizabeth were sitting in the kitchen after dinner. Each was working on their own project when they heard Charlie cry "Mommy!" They both jumped up and ran into the little boy's room. Elizabeth picked him up. He was burning up with a fever. She started to take his pajamas off to cool down when she noticed he had a rash on his stomach and under his arms. It looked like he had the measles.

"I wonder if the Schubert kids were sick when they were here? That's the only way he could have been exposed to them. Do you think we should have Doc Means look at him?"

"Yes, I'll ride into town tomorrow morning and see if he'll come out or if he can tell us what to do. I'll check to see if anyone else in town is sick."

Sure enough there were several cases of measles in town and the doctor was too busy to make the trip to the farm. He told Frank what to watch for and what to do to make the child more comfortable. Frank stopped at the store and bought a lollipop for Charlie. He thought that might make him feel a little better. Matilda Schubert was apologetic.

"Frank I'm so sorry. We didn't know the children were sick when we were at your house for dinner. They all came down with the measles a couple of days later and I've been so busy taking care of them I forgot to warn you. I hope Charlie will be better soon and I hope you and Elizabeth don't get them."

"I had the measles when I was a kid. But I don't know about Elizabeth."

When Frank got home, he found Elizabeth and Lady sitting in Charlie's room. The little dog insisted on staying there. "What did the doctor say?"

"Well, the measles are truly going around. He said that he has his hands full with so many people sick, but he told me what to do for him. He said we should dissolve baking soda in warm water and bathe him in that to help with the itching and to be sure to keep him in a dark room. The light is dangerous for his eyes. By the way, have you had the measles?"

"I don't think so. If I had them when I was little I don't remember, and I don't remember my mother saying anything about them."

"We'll have to watch you. They're worse as you get older."

Charlie continued to be sick for several days and Elizabeth spent every spare moment caring for him. She held him and rocked him and slept with him at night. His fever broke in the middle of the night on the tenth day and he slept through the night for the first time since he'd been sick. He looked pale and worn out but his eyes were bright and alert again.

But Elizabeth felt exhausted and her body ached all over. She hadn't told Frank that she thought she might be pregnant again. She wasn't sure and didn't want to get his hopes up if it was a false alarm. She had to drag herself out of bed and to force breakfast down. She kept going though; mothers don't have the luxury of staying in bed when they're sick. But one morning soon after Charlie was feeling better, she just couldn't force herself to get up. "Oh no" she thought, "this is worse than morning sickness. I feel terrible."

"Frank, wake up, I feel really sick."

"Oh my god, you're really feverish! How long have you been sick?"

"I don't know, I've been feeling a little off for a few days, but now it's gotten the better of me."

Sure enough she had the full blown measles and there was nothing to do but ride it out. She knew it would last for ten days and she dreaded the thought of what was to come.

Frank took such good care of her and Charlie. He was a great nurse – bringing tea and broth to her and making sure Charlie was fed and doing okay. On the fifth day she felt a terrible pain in her abdomen as she tried to get out of bed. When she stood up, she felt something run down her leg and saw a pool of blood at her feet.

"Dear God, I've lost the baby." She sat down on the floor and started to cry.

Frank came in when he heard her crying and when he saw her sitting in the pool of blood, he knew what was wrong. "Oh, Elizabeth - I didn't know. Is there anything I can do? Here let me get you cleaned up and back into bed." He went into the kitchen and brought a basin of warm water to clean her. He helped her into a clean nightgown and mopped the floor. She was so sick and weak she couldn't do anything but lay her head on the pillow and cry.

"I'm so sorry Frank I wasn't sure if I was pregnant and honestly was hoping that I wasn't. Now I've lost our baby and it's all my fault."

"How can you think it's your fault? You didn't do anything to cause this. It's just the way things happen sometimes."

"If I hadn't spent so much time with Charlie maybe I wouldn't have gotten these darned measles."

"If you hadn't spent so much time with your son you wouldn't have been the mother that you are. You did exactly what you should have. He needed you and you took care of him and loved him. You have nothing to apologize for. I love you and I don't blame you for anything. Now, lie back and try to get some sleep. You've got to take care of yourself and get better for us."

Christmas wasn't the happy celebration they'd been hoping for. Charlie was better but was still a little weak and Elizabeth was able to be up and around but was still unable to do much. Doc Means came out to the farm and examined her. He said it looked like everything was all right, that there didn't to appear to be any permanent damage. The Schubert's brought a Christmas dinner out to the family along with some gifts for Charlie and the cameo for Elizabeth. They didn't stay, just brought their gifts and left.

Frank waited a few days until Elizabeth was nearly back to normal and said "Now let's celebrate Christmas. Charlie has no idea what the date is so let's pretend that today's the day."

"That sounds fine. I feel so much better and I don't want to sit around feeling ill any more." She needed something to cheer her up. She'd had too many sad things happen in the past few months.

"Charlie come here. I've got something for you."

"What is it Daddy? What have you got for me?"

"Close your eyes." Frank got the box with the train set in it off the shelf and put it in front of the little boy. "Okay, open them!"

"What's in the box?"

"It's for you. Open it."

"A train! It's a train!!" He took the train cars out of the box and set them on the floor.

"Here, let me show you how it works. You put this little hook in the slot here and it attaches to the next car. Then you can push it around the floor and they all follow. See how the wheels turn?"

"It's like the train Momma and I took to Grampa's. Look Momma, it's a train!" He put the train cars together and pushed them around the floor making chugging sounds. Then he called "Choo, choo!" "See it sounds like a real train too!" He opened and closed all the doors and put his teddy bear on top of the passenger car for a ride. Lady thought it was great fun and chased Charlie as he pushed it around the room.

"That was a hit!" Elizabeth smiled at her boys sitting on the floor playing with the train. She'd asked Frank to get some oranges and apples in town and she'd made both Frank and Charlie some socks but of course the train was the best gift ever.

Frank looked up at her and smiled. "This is for you Mrs. Wagner." He took a little box out of his pocket and handed it to her.

"What's this? I didn't expect anything."

"I hope you like it."

Charlie stopped playing with his train long enough to say "Open it Mommy. Did you get a train too?"

"No, it's not a train, but it's something special just for your Momma."

When she opened the little box, she couldn't believe her eyes. She had seen the cameo in Schubert's store earlier in the year and had admired it. How had he known? "Oh Frank, It's beautiful. I love it. Thank you so much. How did you ever …."

"Don't bother about that, just wear it and look beautiful. Here let me help you put it on your blouse."

He bent over her chair and kissed her. "I'm glad you're feeling better. You really had me worried you know. Merry Christmas and Happy Anniversary – a few days late. I love you."

She laughed. "I almost forgot our anniversary. I love you too. I don't have a special gift for you though."

"Don't worry about that. I've got my wife back- that's enough of a gift for me."

## Chapter

# TWELVE

The next few months were quiet and uneventful. The winter weather kept the family inside most of the time except for the usual chores. Elizabeth spent her evenings working on Lois's wedding dress and Frank always had something to keep his hands busy. Charles was growing so fast he quickly outgrew his clothes. He was learning to recognize letters and loved to draw pictures. Their lives had resumed an orderly, smooth pace.

One morning snow covered the farm yard and the next day things were melting. Spring had arrived bringing with it the promise of a new year - new crops and new babies. The milk cows were pregnant, the laying hens were sitting on their nests and Elizabeth was pretty sure she was expecting again as well. She had the same symptoms as when she had Charlie and the baby she lost. She was worried, but realized that the measles had caused her miscarriage. When she told Frank that she wanted to make an appointment with Doc Means his eyes lit up. "I've been hoping for this. Charlie needs a little brother or sister." The doctor examined her and sure enough she was going to have a baby and everything looked just fine. The baby was due in December so she had all spring and summer to prepare and wait. She wished she could tell her mother, but felt somehow that her mother knew.

The days ran together – there was always so much to do and they fell into bed at night, exhausted. She had never felt better. The Colorado climate truly agreed with her. As spring turned into summer, she couldn't help but keep an anxious eye on the horizon. Thankfully there were no major storms this year. The crops were growing nicely and her garden was too. She would have a bumper crop of corn this year along with tomatoes, cucumbers and squash. She would be very busy for the next few weeks canning and putting up vegetables in the root cellar.

The harvesters had come and gone and Frank was happy with how well his crops had produced. "We should have enough money to buy a bull this year and not have to pay Joe Simpson to bring his over."

"A bull? Aren't they dangerous? I don't want Charlie to be around a bull."

"No, they're not dangerous if you handle them the right way. Any way I'll buy a young one that I can train. If it gets used to being handled and around people it'll be okay. Don't worry, I wouldn't do anything to endanger you or Charlie, and we'll just have to be sure he knows to stay out of the bull's way."

Elizabeth wasn't sure about this new turn of events but trusted Frank. He knew what he was doing when it came to the animals.

True to his word, Frank bought a yearling bull. He was red with a white face – a Hereford – and was very handsome. Frank was proud of him and was sure that this would enable them to increase their cattle herd as well as keep the milk cows fresh. Charlie was interested in the bull and wanted to see him up close. Frank picked him up and took him into the corral with the bull. Charlie petted him on the nose while Frank held him, telling him never to go into to the corral or to try and touch the bull unless he was with him. Lady wasn't going to let that happen either. She was very protective of her little boy. The bull seemed calm and tame but Elizabeth still didn't completely trust him. After all, he was a BULL!! Frank worked with the young bull and soon he was behaving perfectly. He did have a knack with animals. He'd trained Sue and she had grown to be a beautiful mare.

Lois's wedding date was set for the 10<sup>th</sup> of September. She and Frank and Charles would travel to Denver for the event. The crops would be in by then, the garden all harvested and one of the Schubert's sons had agreed to stay at the farm to milk the cows and take care of the livestock for a few days. Elizabeth looked forward to seeing her father and sister even though she would sorely miss her mother. She was anxious for Frank to see all of the motor cars and secretly hoped they could get one someday. She could just see herself driving to town in a car with Charlie bouncing away in the seat next to her.

The wedding was perfect – Lois was a beautiful bride and her dress was lovely. She was beyond appreciative for the beautiful dress and thanked her sister over and over for making it for her. Their sister Sarah and her family came for the wedding as well. The girls hadn't seen each other in several years and their reunion was sweet yet tearful. Memories of their mother were everywhere. Sarah had two boys and they played with Charlie until all three of them were tired out. Frank and Sarah's husband, Ralph, got along well with Jacob and Elizabeth's father. They were all having a wonderful time with their families.

When it was time for everyone to leave, Elizabeth's father called them all together. "I'm going to sell the tailor shop and move back to Arkansas. You all have your own homes and lives now. I still have family back home and have been writing to my sister. She says I can stay with her and her family until I get re-settled there and can start over. I miss your mother every day but think this is the right move for me."

The girls realized that this was the best thing for their father. He had an interested buyer for the shop so it was just a matter of time. His plan was to travel to Elizabeth and Frank's farm on his way to Arkansas, spend some time with them and then go on to Iowa and visit with Sarah and Ralph and her family. That way he could get to know his sons-in-law and his grandchildren. They all thought this was a good plan.

A few weeks later her father pulled into the farmyard with a big wagon loaded with his personal possessions. It was covered with tarps and he looked like a pioneer in a covered wagon.

"Daddy – it's so nice to see you! You've been busy getting everything organized and sold so quickly!" She and Charles ran outside to greet her father.

"Hello Beth, hi there Charlie, how's Grandpa's big boy? I think you've grown three inches since I saw you last. Pretty soon you'll be as big as your daddy." There were hugs all around as they unhitched the horses and put them in the corral with some hay and water.

They went into the house to get out of the wind and have a cup of coffee and a bite to eat. Charlie sat on his grandfather's knee, "Beth, I brought some of your mother's things for you. I gave Lois most of the furniture I didn't have room for in the wagon, but there are quite a few things your mother loved and you might remember.

"Daddy you didn't have to do that, but there are a few things that I have fond memories of and if you don't want them, I'd love to have them."

"Well then, let's take a look."

They went outside and as her father took the covers off the wagon, Charlie hopped around impatiently waiting to see what was in there. "Do you have a dog in there, Grandpa, or a cat? You're going to get pretty lonely on your long trip all by yourself".

"Nope, no dogs or cats Charlie, just a lot of stuff and memories."

He took several boxes out of the wagon and handed one of them to Elizabeth. "This is a picture of your mother and me. We had it taken when we first moved to Denver, right after you started your teaching job. And this box has your mother's china in it, this other one has her silverware. You get first pick. Do you want the china or the silver? There are some crystal candle holders and a candy jar too. Whatever you don't take I'll give to your sister Sarah."

"Let's take these things into the house and sit down to take a look at them."

They carried three of the boxes into the house and set them on the table. Charlie was beside himself with curiosity.

"Is this the picture? I don't remember seeing it at your house, but then both times I've been back things have been hectic to say the least."

She took the picture out of the box. It was oval-shaped, about two feet tall and showed her parents sitting next to each other. Her father was dapper with his hair parted down the middle and his moustache trimmed perfectly. He had on a suit and tie and looked like the businessman that he was. Seeing her mother brought tears to Elizabeth's eyes. She looked so small. Her hair was pulled back into a loose bun. She was wearing a dress with a high collar with her favorite brooch pinned to it. Her face had the sweet expression Elizabeth remembered and loved.

"Thank you so much Daddy. I will cherish this. I know exactly where I'll have Frank hang it. I want it to be in the sitting room where I can see it every day and you and Momma can watch over us. Look Charlie, see Granny and Grandpa? Remember your Granny?"

Her father took out his handkerchief and blew his nose. "I thought you would like it. Your mother looks wonderful don't you think? Now let's take a look at these other boxes."

Charles liked the picture, but was anxious to see what was in the other boxes.

As they opened the other boxes Elizabeth said, "I've always loved both the china and the silverware. They bring back so many memories of our lives in Arkansas. This is going to be a hard decision. Let me think about it. We have dishes that are serviceable but occasionally we have people over for special meals and I don't have enough to serve a big crowd. I think I would like to have the china. I like the way the pink rose twines around the edge of the plates and saucers and seems to cling to the top of the cups. So, yes, I would love to have the china. Sarah will love the silverware too."

"Alright then, the china is yours. What about these other things? Do you want the crystal candle sticks or the candy dish?"

"Candy? Is there candy in that box? I really like candy, Grandpa!"

"No son, there isn't any candy in the box, but if you wait a few minutes I might have a little something in my valise for you." He patted the little boy's head and winked at Elizabeth. "Charles do you know that you're my namesake?"

"What's namesake mean?"

"It means that you and I have the same name."

"But my name's Charles, not Grandpa."

Her father laughed, "That's right your name is Charles and so is mine. Before I was Daddy or Grandpa, I was Charles too. My friends called me Charlie just like your momma calls you Charlie."

"Did your friends call you Charlie Barley? My momma calls me that sometimes."

"No, I don't think anyone ever called me that. That's a pet name your mother has for you because she loves you so much."

Charles laid his head in Elizabeth's lap and she stroked his blond hair. "I love you too Momma."

Her father cleared his throat, "Now, back to the business of the candy jar or the candle sticks. What's your decision?"

"Well, I don't usually keep candy around long enough to make it to a jar, but I do make candles and we use them in the evenings, so I think the candle sticks would be the best choice for us. Thank you again. These are all special memories."

"Oh, one more thing – I'll need Frank to help me with it when he gets home. I want you to have the grandfather clock."

"What?? The big clock that stood in the hallway? Oh my, that's too much! You certainly don't want to part with it do you?"

"I want you to have it, and that's that."

"Daddy, I will think of you every time the clock chimes!" She hugged him and kissed his cheek.

"Well I doubt that, but it's nice to know you've got some good memories."

Later Frank and her father put the clock in the sitting room. It held a place of honor in the corner, where they could see it and hear it as it chimed the hours.

Her father left a couple of days later. He wanted to get on the road before the weather got bad. Before he left, he and Elizabeth took a little walk around her place, just the two of them while Frank kept Charlie busy inside. "Elizabeth, you have become a very capable woman. I always knew you were the strong one, in spite of your health issues. I'm very happy that we made the move to this part of the country and gave you the opportunity to be healthy and have a good life."

"Thank you, Daddy. Sometimes I surprise myself. I used to have to be so careful, but now I'm just a normal person."

"I must say I don't know how you manage to live out here in the middle of nowhere. It's so quiet and lonely and the wind just never stops blowing. You remind me of a ruby or an emerald serenely glowing out here in this windswept place – like a gem in the middle of the prairie." She thought, "That's funny – I've always felt there was a light inside me. I can't believe my father sees it too."

She laughed, "I don't have time to be lonely, with the farm chores and of course Charlie keeps me busy. I wish you could see this place in the spring. It's beautiful then - everything is green when the crops are coming up out of the ground and even the sagebrush is pretty. The sunsets are spectacular and you can see for miles and miles. Of course, the wind blows all of the time but you get used to it. Frank is a good husband and he makes me very happy. I really love my life."

As her father drove the wagon down their lane, she and her family stood in the yard waving and calling to him to have a safe trip. She couldn't help but wonder if she would ever see her father again.

Things were winding down for the winter. She still had some winter vegetables in the garden and of course Charlie always needed to have a hole mended in his pants or his socks. He was growing so fast – he seemed to outgrow his clothes right in front of her eyes. She thought if he stood real still and she watched closely she could see him growing. She laughed to herself, "of course he never stood still for even five minutes". Now it was time to get things organized for the newest member of their family. They were anxious to see if this was going to be another boy or a girl. Time would tell.

October came and went. Frank carved a Jack-o-lantern for Charlie for Halloween which was a big hit. He thought it was kind of scary but funny too. Elizabeth used the pumpkin to make a pie so they all enjoyed the day as they ate pie by the Jack-o-lantern's light. The days were getting shorter and there was frost on the ground in the mornings. It was the time of year when she had the urge to hunker down and get ready for the long, cold winter ahead.

## Chapter

# THIRTEEN

Elizabeth woke with a start. She had been dreaming that her whole body was being pummeled but then she realized it was the baby kicking. This one was a lot more active than Charles had been. It seemed like it never stopped moving. Oh well, she only had a little over a month to go, and then they would be welcoming this new little person into their family.

She hurriedly dressed and braided her long brown hair. Even though Frank had started a fire, it was still chilly in the house. She could hear Charles playing with his train in his room. He was such a good little boy. He would be three in a few weeks. She went to his bedroom door. The sun coming through the window behind him made his blond hair glow.

"You look just like your daddy, Charlie Barley." He smiled and held out his little hands. She sat beside him and kissed him on both cheeks. While she dressed Charles for the day, she heard her husband coming in from the barn with a bucket of milk.

"Good morning family! It's about time you two slackers got your behinds out of those nice warm beds!" He kissed her on the neck and patted her belly. "This one seems like it's just about done cooking in there. Should be here for Christmas?"

Squirming to get down, Charles called, "Daddy, get me, get

me!" Frank pretended not to hear the little boy and then suddenly turned and started to chase him.

"You'd better run, here I come!" Charles ran into the kitchen on his short little legs, laughing and squealing.

"Be careful you two. I don't want any broken furniture or bones in there!" She was always the careful one, the serious one.

As they ate their breakfast Frank said, "It feels like there's a change in the weather this morning. The wind's coming out of the north and it's getting cold. I'm glad we got the hay put up and most of the corn crop harvested. I'm going over to Mrs. Paul's place to finish up. My share of the crop should be enough to feed the cattle for the winter along with the hay."

.

Later, she watched from the kitchen window as Frank put the harness on the horses and hooked them to the wagon. He patted Lady on the head, said something to her, then got into the wagon and turned and blew Elizabeth a kiss as he rode away. The dog followed him for a few feet then turned around and came back to the house.

She buttoned his jacket and put his little red hat and mittens on and said "Okay Charlie Barley, let's go feed the chickens and check for eggs."

"Chickens - I like the chickens!" He loved to chase the rooster.

"I know you do, but you need to stop tormenting that rooster. One of these days he's going to turn around and chase you!"

She hummed a little tune while she worked, filling the feeder and the water trough. She gently lifted the hens to see if there were any eggs. Sure enough there were three eggs. The hens didn't lay as many eggs this time of year, but three was just enough to make a cake for Frank. Today was November 11, 1911, Frank's 30th birthday. 11/11/11 - this was an auspicious date, one that wouldn't happen again for a hundred years. She had knitted a pretty blue scarf for Frank as a surprise for his birthday.

Outside the chicken house she could hear the wind blowing and

Charles laughing as he chased the rooster. When she straightened up, she felt a sharp pain in her lower back. "Charlie" she called, "let's go back to the house and get some milk for the hogs."

"'Kay, Momma here I come. Come on Lady!"

She filled Lady's bowl with milk and carried the bucket to the hog pen. She had to stop and rest on the way. The bucket wasn't heavy, but her back was hurting again. The wind was picking up and it blew her forward as she walked. Lady stayed between Charles and the pig pens. The dog didn't trust the big sows and was especially leery of the boar. The pigs were tame for the most part but if the sows had babies they were very protective. The boar was always dangerous. Elizabeth didn't go into their pens. She poured the milk and grain through the fence into their feed troughs.

"Do you want to stay outside and play with Lady for a while or are you ready to come in?"

"Play with Lady" he replied. He loved the dog and she was always by his side. Frank had fenced off a little yard in front of the house so Charles could safely play and not get into trouble. She opened the gate and the boy and dog went in. Charles found a ball and started tossing it for Lady.

"You two have fun" she called as she closed the gate and went into the cellar. She picked up a sack of flour and hazel eyes. She couldn't wait to be able to wear regular clothes again.

As she put the ingredients for Frank's cake on the kitchen counter and added wood to the cook stove, she thought about the future. Charles had just moved into his "big boy" bed. Frank had built it in his spare time while she had collected soft feathers for the mattress. They would put the new baby in the crib Frank had made for Charles. He was more than a carpenter, Frank was a craftsman.

She felt another twinge in her back, but thought it was from carrying the flour up from the cellar. It couldn't be the baby yet. She wasn't due for more than a month. She held onto the kitchen counter for a minute and then looked out the window to check on Charles. He wasn't in the yard! The gate was open and he and Lady were gone.

She grabbed her coat and ran outside. "Charles! Where are you?" she called. The wind was blowing harder and swallowed her voice. She ran to the chicken house. The chickens had all gone inside out of the cold wind – no Charles. Turning she ran toward the hog pens. The pain in her back brought her to her knees. She got up and ran to the pens – no Charles. She ran to the barn – no Charles.

"Lady!" she called as loudly as she could. "Charleee!" she yelled. The wind was howling out of the north and it was starting to snow.

She looked all around but there was nothing as far as the eye could see. No trees or houses, just miles and miles of prairie. There was a small hill on the west side of their land with a little gully at the base. She started toward the hill and felt another pain. This was stronger than the last one. As she continued toward the gully there was a slight lull in the wind and she thought she heard barking and growling. She hurried on and just before she got to the gully she saw Charlie's red hat caught on a clump of sagebrush, blowing in the wind. She picked it up and ran faster. When she reached the edge of the gully she heard more barking, growling and whining and her little boy crying. She looked over the edge and there he was. Lady was standing between him and three wild dogs. She was trying to keep the dogs at bay as they took turns attacking her. She was holding her right paw up and Elizabeth could see blood running down her leg. Charlie was crying and yelling at the dogs to "GO AWAY!"

"Oh my God" she thought, "What am I going to do?" Frank had always told her not to go out this far without the rifle, and here she was, unarmed, very pregnant and her son was in trouble.

She yelled as loud as she could and looked around for a stick or a rock, anything she could use as a weapon. There was a grove of scrub oak in the bottom of the gully and there were some large branches on the ground. She slid down the side of the gully and landed on her back-side. Her yelling had distracted the dogs. They turned their attention away from Charles and Lady and were concentrating on her. There was a good-sized branch within arm's reach and she leaned over to grab it. As she did, the biggest of the dogs charged her, teeth bared and snarling. Lady tried to stop him but the other two dogs went after her. All Elizabeth could think was to protect her child.

She swung the branch as hard as she could and connected with the big dog's snout. He yelped and turned away momentarily, then came back and mounted a fresh attack. She hit him again and again until he wasn't moving.

She said "Charlie lie down on the ground and curl up real tight. Put your head down toward your tummy like a roly-poly bug and stay that way. OK?" She hoped that would protect his face and chest if the other dogs attacked.

The other two dogs had stopped fighting with Lady for the moment and when Elizabeth yelled and approached them with her branch they turned and ran. Apparently the big one was their leader. She called to Lady and the brave little dog limped over to her. Elizabeth checked the dog's leg. It looked like it might be broken. Lady had cuts on her head and nose and her left ear was bleeding, but she was alert. She hugged Lady and thanked her for protecting her son. Elizabeth was trembling. She had never experienced such pure rage and the aftermath made her feel weak. Her arms and shoulders ached from beating the dog and slowly she crumpled to the ground. As she sat in the shelter of the gully trying to get her breath, another pain hit her. This was the worst so far and she realized that her water had broken while she had fought with the dog. It wasn't going to be long before she would be in full-blown labor and need help.

She tried to stand and had to use the branch to get to her feet. She called, "Charles, its okay the dogs are gone, but we need to get back to the house now." She held out her arms for the boy and he ran to her. She checked him over and found that he had a cut on his head and his hands were scratched from falling into the gully, but luckily, he hadn't been bitten by the dogs. She brushed the dirt off of his coat, put his hat back on his little head and put the one remaining mitten on his hand. Together they climbed out of the gully. She was able to push him up a little at a time and follow him, but had to stop every few minutes to let another pain pass. Lady limped up behind them on her three good legs.

When they finally reached the top of the gully the wind hit them like a freight train. The snow was blowing sideways and she couldn't see more than a few feet ahead of her. Her brave little boy started crying. He was cold and his tears were freezing on his cheeks. She wanted to cry too, but knew that wouldn't do anyone any good.

"Its okay baby" she crooned, "we're okay now. Just be Momma's big boy and keep walking toward home."

The three of them slowly made their way through the sage brush and tried to avoid the blowing tumble weeds. Eventually she could see the outline of their big barn and felt a surge of adrenaline that pushed her on. Just as she reached the side of the barn, she felt an immense urge to push. "Oh, dear God," she thought, "I cannot have this baby out here in the open. I have to get to shelter, even if it's in the barn."

The weary trio struggled to get up the big step into the barn. Elizabeth lifted Charles first, and then turned to help Lady. It was dark in the barn, but it was out of the wind and relatively warm. Soon her eyes adjusted to the dim light but she had no energy to get up and move out of the barn walkway. Her skirt was frozen stiff from her water breaking and her legs felt like icicles. The urge to push was starting again. She had no control over this impulse. She wondered where Frank was and hoped he had found shelter somewhere.

"God, please help me. I don't know if I can do this by myself" she said out loud.

"Bethy, you've had a baby and you know what to do. Just be calm and keep your wits about you." It was her mother's voice.

"Mother? Is that you?" It had been a little over a year since her mother had passed away and Elizabeth thought about her and missed her every day.

"Find a blanket and something to bind and cut the cord. You can do this Bethy."

The urge to push had passed for the moment. She struggled to her feet and went into the storage room. She found a horse blanket. There was Frank's big knife hanging on a hook and on a shelf sat a ball of twine.

She took everything into the vacant stall where they stored clean straw for bedding for the cows. She put the blanket on top of a pile of straw and lay down to wait for the next pain.

"Momma?" Charles was watching her from the door of the stall.

"Oh honey. Why don't you go find Callie? Her kittens should have their eyes open. If you're very gentle you can pick them up and pet them.

He ran down the walkway. He was back in an instant. "Momma, there's two yellow ones, a gray one and a black one. Can we keep the black one? Please?"

"We'll see. You go and play with them for a little while. OK?"

"OK".

Lady sat next to Elizabeth holding her paw off the ground, whining. "Oh Lady, I'm so sorry. I'll take care of you in just a little...."

"Oh God!" Here it comes!

The baby was born in a gush of water and blood onto the blanket. She picked it up and saw that it had a white caul over its head and it wasn't breathing. She removed the white sac from the baby's face and held it up by its feet. She gave the baby a shake and hit it on the back. Nothing. She put her own mouth against the baby's tiny mouth and blew air into the little lungs. Suddenly the baby jerked its arms and started to cry. She opened her coat and blouse and held the baby against the warmth of her breast and cried too. She felt another urge to push and delivered the placenta. She grabbed the knife and cut a piece of twine, then tied the twine around the umbilical cord to stop the bleeding and cut the cord. Exhausted she lay back on the straw and wrapped her arms around the tiny baby.

"Thank you, God and thank YOU Mother."

"Momma, what's that?" She wondered how long he'd been standing there and hoped he hadn't seen anything too disturbing.

"Well, let's see. I think it's your new little sister!" She looked closer at the baby. "Yes, it is a little sister. Do you want to look at her?"

"No, she's all red and wet. Are her eyes open yet?"

Elizabeth smiled. "Well not really open but they will be soon."

"What's her name?"

"I don't know yet. Your daddy and I will have to decide, but I think it might be Mary after your grandma."

"Oh, I want to name the black kitten Cinders. He looks like he got into the cinders in the stove." He came and sat beside her on the straw and laid his head on her breast next to the baby and fell sound asleep.

She felt another twinge and realized she was feeling another urge to push. What was going on? Then she realized there was another baby waiting to be born! Twins! She was having twins. That's why they had come early there were two of them.

Within a matter of minutes, she gave birth to another little girl. She knew what to do this time and soon the baby was nestled next to her sister and big brother in the crook of Elizabeth's arm. Charles had slept through the whole thing. His ordeal must have exhausted him.

Suddenly Lady started to bark her happy bark. Frank must be outside. Thank God! The barn door opened and a gust of cold air and snow preceded her husband into the barn.

"What the, Beth, what's going on here? Why are you in the barn? Oh my God, what's all this blood? Are you okay?"

Charles woke when he heard his father's voice.

"Daddy! I have a new little sister and her name's Mary and she's all red and wet and Momma said I can keep the black kitten!"

"Oh Frank I'm so glad you're here. I'll explain all this later. I just need to get to the house and Lady needs to be tended to." Elizabeth was incredibly tired and relieved and so, so happy to see her husband.

Frank picked her and the babies up and carried them into the house and put them in their bed. After the babies were clean and wrapped in nice warm blankets she fell into a deep, dreamless sleep.

Later after Frank had taken care of Lady and done the chores, she explained what had happened. He said "I'm just glad they didn't bite you or Charlie, they're probably sick. I hope Lady's okay."

They had a quiet moment to get to know the newest members of their family. One baby had soft blond fuzz on her head, the other had a shock of dark hair.

"Frank let's name them Mary and Margaret after our mothers. Would that be okay with you?"

"Of course, I love both names." He smiled and kissed both babies on their little heads.

Elizabeth smiled, "Oh, happy birthday! This isn't quite what I had planned for your birthday gift. I do have another little something for you. Look up there on the shelf wrapped in tissue. It matches your eyes and will keep you warm this winter."

"Happy birthday, Daddy, I have a present for you too!" Charles reached into his pocket and pulled out an arrowhead. I found it behind the chicken house. Lady and I were looking for more when we got lost."

"Well, thank you both very much. November 11, 1911 has been a day I'll never forget." He wrapped the scarf around his neck and sat down. He picked Charles up and put him on his lap, "But, Charlie, you must never, ever wander away like that again. You could have gotten really lost or hurt and poor Lady did get hurt protecting you."

"I know. I'm sorry Daddy. I won't ever do that again."

"Now, don't cry, just don't do it again." He wiped the child's face, "Kiss Momma and your sisters good night."

"Good night Charlie, I love you!"

"Love you too, Momma."

After Charles was settled into his bed Frank came back into the room. "I'll ride Sue into town tomorrow if the weather clears and bring Doc Means out to check on you and the babies."

"Okay, I really don't want you to leave, but we need birth certificates at the very least." Elizabeth was so very tired that she could barely keep her eyes open.

Frank turned the wick down on the oil lamp. When he got into bed, he took her into his arms and held her close. "I love you Elizabeth Wagner."

"And I love you too Frank Wagner." This had been a day to remember. She felt safe and warm and incredibly happy as she fell asleep. That gem inside her was glowing!

The next few years went by like a whirlwind. The girls were as different as night and day. Mary had Elizabeth's dark hair and Frank's blue eyes and would rather wear overalls than a dress. She was a tom-boy and she loved taking care of the animals. Her favorite thing was to follow Charles around. He took his role as "big brother" seriously but got tired of her constant chatter and incessant questions. Margaret was blond with hazel eyes and loved to stay in the house with Elizabeth. She liked to help in the kitchen and learned to sew at an early age. Both girls liked to ride Sue and as they got older, the three of them, Charlie, Mary and Margaret could be seen riding around the ranch laughing and having fun. They were careful to stay close to the house and not to bother the cattle, especially the big bull.

Frank planned to buy a buggy for the children to take to the school house a few miles away. He was bartering with one of their neighbors and had already started to train Sue to pull a cart. The whole family could ride to town on Sundays for church in a buggy rather than in the big wagon.

Charlie was six and the twins were three when Elizabeth had their second son, James. It was an easy pregnancy and both Charles and Frank were happy to have another boy in the family. Their house was bursting at the seams and Frank announced one morning that he was going to add another couple of rooms. They needed another bedroom and a bigger sitting room would be nice. They could put the kitchen table in the current sitting room and that would give Elizabeth a lot more room in the kitchen. Elizabeth was all for this idea. There was hardly enough room to walk around the beds in the children's room and of course their toys were all over the house. Apparently, he'd been thinking about this for some time because he had the plans all ready and he started working on the addition as soon as the harvesters had come and gone.

It was good experience for Charles - he was Frank's main helper. He watched his father as he built the foundation, the walls and put the roof on. His main job was to "hold the other end" of whatever Frank was working on, to steady the ladder and to fetch tools. Frank made a point of praising him in the evenings over supper. Of course, Mary wanted to help too and ran her little legs off "helping" her father and brother. The addition was nearly complete by Christmas. It just needed to be finished on the inside and the walls painted and they could move in to the new bedroom and sitting room. Margaret helped Elizabeth make curtains for the new rooms and they braided new rag rugs for the floors while baby James sat in his crib and watched them. The house was a beehive of activity and Elizabeth had never been happier. Their lives weren't exciting but they were content.

James was a beautiful baby. He had Frank's blond hair and blue eyes and his ready smile lit up the room. All of the children loved him and competed to see who could make him laugh. He was the center of attention at home and in town when they made their weekly trips to sell eggs and cream. People would stop them to comment on how precious he was. He came to expect the attention.

By the time he was a year old he was walking and saying a few words. He imitated his brother and sisters and tried to keep up with them. He toddled after them where ever they went. Charles was the leader of course, and the girls would take turns carrying him when he got tired. Elizabeth watched from the kitchen window as her family ran around, chasing the roosters and playing with Lady. She loved the way they got along and the contrast in their appearance was amazing.

Charles started school that fall. Elizabeth had worked with him – teaching him his letters and numbers. She wanted him to do well sort of as a reflection on her teaching abilities. The girls liked to sit with them and draw pictures and listen as he worked on his lessons or read from his primer. James always wanted to sit with them too, but wanted to be on top of the table, taking pencils and dropping paper and just being a general nuisance.

"Jimmy! Stop it. That was my best picture!" Mary whined.

"Okay, get down now. If you can't be careful with your sisters' things you can't be up here." Elizabeth picked the toddler up and set him on the floor. Pretty soon he was climbing back up on a chair and trying to get back on the table. He was so cute that he got away with things – with a little grin over his shoulder he was off to get into something else.

Their weeks became months and then the months turned into years and soon the girls were old enough to go school too. That left James and Elizabeth at home alone. Jimmy loved being the center of Elizabeth's world. The only problem was that she was expecting baby number five and then he would have to share the lime light. He kept her and Lady busy running after him. One morning she looked out the kitchen window and saw something near the top of the windmill in the corral. "Oh my god, is that Jimmy up there?" Sure enough, there he was climbing the ladder looking off in the distance.

"James!! What are you doing up there? You get down right now. No wait, don't jump I'm coming to help you!" She was beside herself. "What ever possessed you to climb up there?"

"I wanted to see Daddy working in the field and I think I can see the school house. I want to go to school too."

She knelt down and held him to her breast. "You scared me to death Jimmy. You could have fallen and broken your arm or even your neck. Don't ever do that again – OK?"

"I'm a big boy Momma. I wasn't a bit afraid and I liked to see everything."

"Well, if you do that again I will cut a willow switch and you'll be sorry. Your father will not think this was funny!" That seemed to scare him and he promised not to do it again. She wasn't sure if she believed him, and made a mental note not to leave him unattended in the farm yard for awhile.

A few weeks later she saw him playing in the yard Frank had fenced around the house. He was swinging something around. It looked like a rope but when she got closer, she saw that it was a snake skin with rattles attached to the end. "Where did you find this?"

"Oh, it was over there stuck in the fence. It's neat isn't it?"

"Yes, it is neat, but don't touch things like this without asking your father or me. Did you see the snake that used to live in this skin?'

"Nope, it was just there stuck in the fence all by itself. The things on the end make noise when I swing it. Watch!"

"Those are rattles. This skin belonged to a rattle snake. You remember Daddy and me telling you about rattle snakes, don't you? They are very, very dangerous and if you see one run the other way as fast as you can."

"I can kill a rattle snake. I'm a big boy. I just need a big knife."

"You don't need a knife and don't you even think about trying to kill any kind of snake. Snakes are not something you want to tangle with. Even the bull snakes have a job so just leave any snake you might see alone. Okay? Promise me."

"Yes…." He hung his head and scuffed his toe in the dirt.

She knelt down beside him, "Oh honey, I don't want you to get hurt, that's all."

"I know. I was just having fun."

"Come on, let's go inside and have a cookie."

"Okay, I love cookies!!"

When Frank came in for dinner, she told him about the snake skin incident. "James, come here. Your mother tells me you found a snake skin. Do you know where that skin came from? Well, once a year a snake sheds its skin and grows a new one. Sort of like when Lady sheds her coat in the summer. My father always said you could tell how old a snake was by the number of rattles on its tail. This skin you found today has ten rattles on it so that means the snake is probably ten years old. That's even older than Charles. So, if you see one of them again, let your mother or me know, but you don't touch it okay? I'll make a necklace for you out of these rattles that you found today."

"Isn't a necklace for girls?"

"Well, sometimes boys wear special necklaces made of rattles. I used to have one when I was a boy."

"You did? How many rattles did it have? Where did you find it? What happened to it?"

"It was a pretty old snake. It had at least twelve rattles. I found it out in the pasture at the farm I grew up on. I don't know what happened to it, I probably lost it or it broke or something. The point is, don't touch things like that without telling your mother or me."

"Is there anything we can do to keep him safe?" Elizabeth asked.

"All we can do is to try and make him understand how dangerous things like that can be."

Elizabeth delivered a baby girl a few weeks later. This was her fifth child and she was planning on it being her last. The baby was healthy and beautiful of course, but she had her hands full with the other four, especially with James. Charles was nine, the girls were six and James was three. They were all special in their own way and she loved them all equally. As she lay in her bed holding this newest little bundle, Frank said. "I would like to name her Emily. My father's mother's name was Emily and she was very special to me."

"Of course, we can name her Emily. You've never talked about your grandmother. Did you live near her when you were growing up?"

"Yes, she lived with us and took care of us when my mother passed away. She was more like a mother than a grandmother. There were four of us boys and she certainly had her hands full with us.

She didn't tolerate any nonsense, but she loved us. Our mother died having our baby sister. The baby died and our father was never the same."

"Oh Frank. I've often wondered what happened to your mother and father."

"I don't like to talk about it, actually none of us do. We just got on with our lives and didn't take the time to feel sorry for ourselves. Grandma Emily helped us get over losing our mother and helped our father get back on track with his life. They're all buried in Nebraska on the farm we grew up on."

"Well I hope little Emily here can live up to the wonderful woman she's named for."

Frank leaned over and kissed Elizabeth and the baby and went to check on the other little ones. Elizabeth closed her eyes and fell into a deep, blissful sleep.

## Chapter

# *FIFTEEN*

Elizabeth, James and Emily were alone at the farm. The other children were at school and Frank was working in the field. She sat in the rocker, nursing Emily. The weather had gotten warm, spring was in the air and the crops were starting to come up. She hadn't heard James for a few minutes and wondered where he was and what he'd gotten into this time. She finished feeding the baby, put her into her cradle and went to look for her son.

He wasn't in his room. That's where he'd been when she sat down to feed the baby. She opened the door and called, "Jimmy. Where are you?" No answer. "JAMES! Where ARE you??"

She went outside and called again. Still no answer. She grabbed her coat and started toward the barn, calling his name as she went. Maybe he'd gone to see the new kittens. There was no sign of him anywhere. "Oh my goodness, where has that child gotten to?" she thought.

She found him sitting behind the barn crying and holding his little hand in his lap. Lady sat next to him, whining. "What happened? Are you alright?"

"No, I got hurt Momma. I found a big snake laying on a flat rock in the sun. I just wanted to look at it and count how many rattles it had and see if I could make a necklace and the snake bit me."

"What?? The snake bit you? Where did it bite you? Oh my god, it bit you on the hand didn't it?"

His hand was swollen and turning purple. She picked him up and ran to the house. He was crying in earnest now. She ran into the kitchen and took her sharpest paring knife out of the knife block. She made two slits next to the bite and started to suck the venom out of his hand. He cried and tried to pull his hand away. He said "I'm sorry Momma." She tied a rag around his wrist hoping to keep the venom from moving up his arm. She ran to the barn and hitched Sue up to the buggy, put the baby in her traveling basket and carried her and James out to the buggy.

She drove as fast as she could to the field where Frank was working. When he saw her coming, he knew something was terribly wrong. By the time she'd gotten to him he was off the plow and running toward her. "What's wrong?? What's happened??"

"Frank, James has been bitten by a rattler!"

"What?? How did this happen?"

"I was feeding Emily and he went outside without my knowing it I called him and went outside to look for him. I found him behind the barn holding his hand. I cut it and tried to get the venom out, but I think I was too late." The child was lying in the back of the buggy, moaning but not responding to them.

Frank turned the work horses loose in the field and got into the buggy and they drove into town. Emily was in her basket in the back of the buggy and Elizabeth held James on her lap, hoping to give him strength to fight against the venom. They stopped at the school house and got the other children and went to the doctor's office. By the time they got there, James was unconscious. His hand was swollen to twice its size and was purple and hot to the touch. Frank swept him up and ran into the doctor's office, while she and the other children followed.

After a few minutes, the doctor came out of the examining room. "I'm so sorry but there was nothing I could do. He's gone.

Elizabeth you did the right thing by cutting above the bite, but he's so little that the snake's venom was too strong for his body."

She fell to her knees sobbing. Frank was crying too and so were the other children. How could this have happened? They were so sure he understood how dangerous snakes can be. Three-year old boys are not supposed to die like this....

Of course, she blamed herself for not watching him closely enough and Frank blamed himself for telling him about the rattle necklace. When in reality it was no one's fault. It was just a horrible accident and a terrible fact of life for people who make their living on the land.

Elizabeth had barely been aware of what was going on at the child's funeral. She couldn't sleep or eat. She hadn't bathed or washed her hair for weeks. She was barely functioning, barely feeding the baby. Frank had been taking care of the other children. But she knew she had to snap out of this depression and take care of her family. She came out of her fugue long enough to take a look at herself in the mirror and couldn't believe what she saw. She looked like an old woman. Her hair had turned completely white. "Frank, why didn't you tell me? I've aged twenty years."

"I barely noticed it myself Elizabeth. I've just been hanging on trying to keep things together."

"I don't know what we're going to do. We've lost our baby, our second son. My heart feels like it's broken."

"I know, mine feels broken too, but we've got to take care of our other babies. They need us, they need you. I was raised without a mother and I know how hard that is. We have to be strong for them and hope God will help us get through this."

"I'm not sure I even believe in God. How could He let this happen? James was just an innocent little boy!"

"I don't have any answers right now. I just know that we've got to get through this together some how."

They went into the other room where the other children were just sitting staring out the windows. When she saw their faces, she felt so guilty. They looked like little abandoned orphans. They had lost their baby brother and it seemed like they had lost their mother too. They were just as sad as she and Frank were. She sat in her rocker and held out her arms to them. They all crowded around her and she held them while they all cried. Frank held the baby and cried along with them. This was the biggest challenge they'd had and they all needed every ounce of strength they could muster to deal with it. Their lives would never be the same. They would never forget that beautiful, fearless little boy and there would always be an empty space in their hearts but they had to rebuild their lives for their family's sake.

The gem had gotten very dim, but was still there in her heart.

# SIXTEEN

"Well, the first order of business here is water. Frank we're going to need a lot of water. First we all need baths and clean clothes. I'll take the sheets off all the beds. Let's get started."

The children ran around in circles taking their clothes off as they ran – their mother was back! Frank started to fill buckets with water while Elizabeth started a fire in the wood stove to heat it up. Life must go on – she had to be there for her family.

Frank was the strong one this time, but he was beginning to worry that he would have to do this all alone and it was more than one person could do, especially at this time of year. The fields needed to be plowed and the crops planted, the garden tilled and planted too. Spring was a busy time of year and he had four growing children to tend to as well as the livestock. He breathed a huge sigh of relief when Elizabeth came back to her senses. He needed her – more than she would ever know. Maybe their lives would get back to some sort of normal. It would never be the same, but they couldn't just stop living.

Elizabeth stripped the sheets off the beds and threw them in the wash tub. Just bathing and washing her hair seemed to give her a new lease on life. She felt better immediately. Frank and the children were all clean and dressed in clean clothes and they looked so much better. The laundry was drying on the clothesline outside as she put some bread in the oven.

"These poor little things haven't had a decent meal since the funeral." The funeral – remembering the funeral almost brought her to her knees, but she pulled herself together and got on with what she should be doing. "I can't let myself go back there to that dark place. I have to be strong."

Charlie was sweeping the floors while Margaret washed the dishes and Mary dried them. The house was taking on a semblance of normalcy. Frank came in carrying an armload of firewood for the stove, Lady was at his heels.

"Something smells delicious in here" he said.

"Is any body hungry?" she called.

"YES!" They all yelled as one.

"Okay, wash up and let's eat this beef stew."

They bowed their heads and thanked God for their blessings before they ate. Elizabeth was still holding a grudge against God and found it hard to thank him for anything. Frank looked at her as she lifted her head and took her hand in his. "It will be alright I promise."

"I know I just need some time to heal."

They were all so busy getting things back in order and the spring chores done that none of them had time to mourn or grieve. That was a good thing and soon their lives were back to a new kind of normal.

One morning she awoke with an old familiar feeling – nausea, lethargy and a slight dizziness. "Oh no, I don't' think I can do this again. Emily is only a year old, and I'm not ready for another baby."

When she told Frank, he said he felt that this child was a blessing. It would never replace James, but might help ease the pain of losing him. She wasn't so sure. James had only been gone for a few months and the loss was still like a sharp pain in her heart every day.

The months went by and her family thrived even with the loss of their brother. Children are resilient and they were looking forward to meeting the new baby. Emily wasn't really aware of what was happening but knew things were okay.

The first of the year brought another baby to the Wagner household. Elizabeth gave birth to a healthy baby boy in February of 1919. They named him Joseph. He looked just like Charlie had when he was born – blond and blue-eyed. Elizabeth thought "He is a pretty baby, just not quite as beautiful as James had been." Then she realized that she absolutely could NOT compare him to her lost son. It wasn't fair to anyone especially Joseph. The rest of the family was ecstatic to have a new little person and things settled into a nice, easy routine once again.

The months went by – winter turned into spring and spring into summer. Joseph was a quiet, content baby. He was happy to watch his brother and sisters and didn't seek to be the center of attention. They all loved him and Charles was especially happy to have a little brother. Elizabeth hoped their lives would continue to be simple and easy. Time would tell. That gem was starting to glow again.

## Chapter

# SEVENTEEN

The years had been good to them. Frank was able to buy Mrs. Paul's property as well as several other parcels of land. They'd bought a tractor a few years earlier and Frank had retired Nick and Jack. The kids rode them to school or to pull the wagon. Their herd of cattle had increased until they had to buy another bull. Elizabeth still had her chickens, but Frank had to build her a much bigger chicken house to hold them all. She'd added ducks and a few geese to her flock. The geese were a pain but the eider down was wonderful for making pillows and mattresses. The ducks were just fun to have around and they laid delicious eggs. They had four milk cows now. They needed the extra milk just to feed their family and to have a little cream left over to sell. The older kids helped with the milking. Farming was a family affair.

The children were growing too fast. Charles was in high school. He went to school in town and they only saw him on the weekends. It was much easier in the winter to have him stay in town. They didn't want to worry about him coming home every day in bad weather. He boarded with the Schubert family where Elizabeth had stayed when she first came to Hartford. It seemed like a hundred years ago. Wilbur and Matilda had more or less retired and their oldest son Willy, had taken over their mercantile business. They were still a big part of Frank and Elizabeth's lives.

At sixteen, Charles had grown to be even taller than Frank. He was still as blond as ever with clear, intelligent blue eyes and was a strikingly handsome young man. Elizabeth noticed that several of the girls in town seemed very interested in her oldest son. He wanted to go into farming with his father and was always reading about new ways of doing things that would improve the crops and the livestock production. Frank would listen patiently to him and would promise to "try that new method soon." But Charlie's first love was their Model T Ford. They bought it in Denver from Lois's husband, Jacob. Jacob was not only fixing cars he was selling them too. Charles loved to tinker with the car, polish it, and especially loved to drive it. Elizabeth could see him coming for a mile, there was such a huge dust cloud following him. Luckily the car couldn't go very fast, but it was still in danger of sliding off the dirt roads or tipping over, so he was only allowed to drive to the mailbox or to the field where his father was working to take him a snack.

Frank always drove them into town. He liked driving the car just as much as Charlie did. He would get the crank and start the engine while he waited for his family to come out. Then he'd walk around the machine, kicking tires and making sure everything was in good working order. Once everyone was inside, he'd shout "Hang on to your hats family! We're going to town!!" They'd all laugh and squeal and away they would go.

Elizabeth loved driving the car too. She would take it to town every couple of weeks to do her trading and to bring Charles a little treat of some kind. She was a careful driver especially when she had one of the children with her. She missed Charlie and took every opportunity she could to go to town and visit him. She hoped that when he was old enough to really know what he wanted to do with his life, it would keep him close to them. She secretly hoped he'd buy a place near them so she could see him as often as she wanted.

The twins were teenagers. Hard to believe, but they were thirteen and still as different as night and day. They were both looking forward to the day when they were in high school and could stay in town too. There were a lot more fun things to do in town than on the farm. There was a moving picture theater and of course the Sweet Shoppe and dime store were always full of kids.

Margaret was more of a homebody than her sister and was an amazing pianist. Frank had gone to school to pick the children up and found her sitting in the school house playing the piano. She had a natural talent and when he saw the look of pure joy on her face Frank had asked Mr. Schubert to order a piano for her. She had just turned ten and had spent every spare moment playing it since then. Both girls had inherited their musical ability from their father and the three of them loved to sing together in the evenings while Elizabeth knitted and tapped her toe. Music was Maggie's life and she wanted to become a professional musician when she grew up. She liked to perform and knew she was a vision to behold with her long, blond hair shining as she played and sang. She would finish her performance with a lovely little flourish, toss her hair and daintily curtsy and bow to her audience - which up to this point consisted mostly of her family. Her natural shyness disappeared when she sat down at the piano. She and Mary harmonized beautifully and lately had been asked to perform at various functions at school and church. Mary went along just to keep her sister company.

Mary loved the animals, especially the horses. She was a dare-devil and loved to do tricks on Sue's back. "Watch this!" she'd yell as she rode by at break-neck speed. Elizabeth held her breath and tried not to look. Mary could get Sue to do anything, from kneeling to rearing on her hind legs. So far she hadn't broken any bones, but it seemed like it was just a matter of time. She was as pretty as Margaret only her hair was dark. She liked it short and looked adorable in her trendy little bob. Elizabeth tried not to be overprotective but every time Mary would do some insane trick she would remember James and his fearlessness. Mary's dream was to go to Hollywood and ride in the movies. Since they'd opened the moving picture theater in town she was enthralled. "I can do that stuff, and I can do it even better than those dudes in the movies do it." She talked non-stop all the way home about the cowboys in the movies and the horses. Frank and Elizabeth were skeptical to say the least.

"I'll bet Maggie could get a job playing the piano for the movies that I'll star in."

"Oh brother, that'll be the day that I'll sit in a dark old movie theater and play the piano while you ride around being a "star". I've got bigger plans than that! By the way Mother, when I go to school in town I'd like to be in the marching band. Do you think I can do that?"

"Oh Mom, I want to be a cheerleader when we go to school in town. I can do three cartwheels in a row without stopping, and I have a really loud voice to lead the cheers."

"You can't wear those stupid overalls when we're in high school silly. And you can't do cartwheels in a dress – your holey underwear will show. But you do have a very loud, annoying voice."

"My underwear isn't holey and besides the cheerleaders at school wear special trousers, don't they Mom?"

Elizabeth laughed, "Yes, I suppose you can be in the school marching band Maggie, and yes I imagine you can be a cheerleader Mary, if in fact they do allow them to wear trousers. We'll just have to wait and see, you've got a couple more years to think about these things. And Margaret, don't be so snide with your sister it isn't becoming."

As he drove the car, Frank glanced over at Elizabeth sitting in the passenger seat and gave her a look that meant "we've got an interesting time ahead of us!" She reached over Joseph who was sitting in the middle and squeezed Frank's hand as if to say "yes we do – hang on tight!"

"Emily, come eat dinner." At seven, she was the serious one of the family. She spent a lot of time in her room doing her homework or drawing at the little desk Frank had built her. She had inherited Frank's artistic ability and Elizabeth's love of learning. She always strived for perfection in everything she did. She was a pretty little girl, but in a more reserved way than her sisters. Her hair wasn't as light as Margaret's or as dark as Mary's but somewhere in between, it was more of a honey color. She was Elizabeth's constant companion. She liked the mathematics of baking – being sure to measure everything correctly to get the right result. But she really loved to knit. The counting and the precision intrigued her and she especially liked mixing colors and making her own intricate patterns. Her projects were works of art and Frank had made several special racks so she could hang them on the walls like paintings. She liked the piano too, the rhythms and the way the notes came together to make a song were fascinating to her. Everything in her world revolved around numbers. She even made her own crossword puzzles and shared them with her friends at school. Her mother had made an exception and had let her have a kitten in her room. She loved their dog, but a cat was a less demanding companion. Her kitten would sit in her lap purring for hours on end while she made her creations. She wasn't looking forward to the day when the twins would move to town for the winter, but wouldn't mind having a room all to herself during the week. The constant squabbling got tiresome. She liked peace and quiet.

"I'm coming Momma. I just want to finish this last math problem, then I'll be done with my homework."

"Emmy you look pale. You need to get some fresh air and sunshine. Do your eyes hurt? They look red."

"I'm fine, I'll go outside after we eat, okay? I'll help with the chores. My eyes are okay, but sometimes it's hard to see things that are real small."

"Maybe we should have Doc Ralston take a look at your eyes. You might need glasses."

"Oh no! I don't want to wear glasses! They're just a pain and I'll look ugly!"

"They might help you knit and do your artwork. We'll just see what the doctor has to say. You don't have to worry about being ugly either, you're a pretty little girl no matter what, and there's more to a person than their looks anyway."

"Momma you're just saying that to make me feel better."

"Who's ugly?" Joseph walked in with the new puppy.

"Stay out of this, we weren't talking to you little brother!"

"What's got you so upset? I was just asking a question. Come on Lucy, let's go find a ball." He and the puppy went back outside.

"Emily, don't be so touchy. There's nothing to do about it, if you need glasses you need glasses and, in the end, it'll be the best thing."

"Hold on Joe, we're going to eat dinner in a few minutes. Put the puppy in the yard so she won't get in any trouble while you eat, then come and wash your hands and face."

Joseph was the baby of the family, the quiet one. He was easygoing but somehow seemed to know that he had a big pair of shoes to fill. It didn't seem to bother him – if anything he seemed to make a point of being the opposite of the way he thought James had been. He'd heard all the stories about the brother that he never knew. He missed Charles, his big brother was his hero and Charles took that role very seriously. He was always patient with his little brother.

Frank spent as much time with the little boy as possible, but as they acquired more land he spent more and more time working. Joe was Frank's shadow when he worked around the place. He was always one step behind, running to catch up with his father's big steps.

Now he had something to keep him occupied. Lady was fifteen years old and was having trouble getting around. She was retired and spent her days sleeping by the stove. One day Frank came home with another Border Collie. When he took the new puppy out of the car, Joe's eyes lit up. He ran up to his father and Frank put the little bundle of fur in his arms.

"Be careful, she's just a baby. You have to be very gentle with her. She'll probably be your dog, so you can pick her name.'

"She's beautiful! I love her. I'll take real good care of her. I think she looks like her name should be Lucy, I'm going to name her Lucy. Is that okay?"

"Sure, if that's what you think, that's fine with me. Go show her to your mother and the girls and Lady. They'll be surprised don't you think?"

"Momma, look what Daddy brought home! Isn't she pretty? I'm going to call her Lucy. Daddy said I could name her."

"Just look at her, yes, she is pretty. Look even Lady likes her.:" Lady got up from her bed by the stove and was checking the new puppy. "You'll have to ask Daddy and Charlie to show you how to train her. They did a good job with Lady, and she'll probably help too."

The girls loved the puppy too, but sure enough she was Joe's dog and she was always at his side. She seemed to know she had big paws to fill too. Elizabeth watched from the kitchen window as they played in the yard. It reminded her of when Charles was a little guy and how Lady was his best friend. Those were such good memories.

## Chapter

# EIGHTEEN

Frank and Elizabeth were driving to Ft. Collins to take supplies to Charles. He was in his last year at Colorado Agricultural College and had moved out of the dorm and into a small house off campus. He was doing very well in school and seemed to have found his niche in life. They were all looking forward to his graduation and the time when he would come back to Hartford and take up farming with his father. There were several options available to him nearby if he wanted to take on a farm of his own but in the meantime the plan was for him to live with them, work with Frank and save enough money to get a good start. Well, they thought that was the plan.

They drove up to the address he sent them and were surprised to see a strange car in the driveway of the house. When they went up to the door and knocked a lovely young woman answered the door. "Hello, you must be Charlie's parents. We've been expecting you. I'm Laura Daniels, Charlie's friend. Please come in. I'm just helping him get settled."

Elizabeth and Frank were speechless for a moment. They looked at each other and back at the girl and asked, "Is Charles here?"

"Mom, Dad, I see you've met Laura." Charles came to the front door from the back of the house. "Come on in, here let me take your coats. What's in the box? Did you have a good trip?"

"Hello Charlie." There were hugs all around. They weren't sure what they should do or how to handle the situation. Were Charles and Laura a couple? He hadn't mentioned anything about a girlfriend when he was home for the summer. They had a lot of questions. Charles and Frank went out to the car to get the rest of the things they'd brought for Charlie's house.

"Mrs. Wagner, can I get you a cup of coffee or something? I think Charles has some cups and a coffee pot somewhere in this mess."

"That would be lovely. We left early this morning so yes a cup of coffee would be wonderful." Elizabeth sneaked a peek at the girl as she looked for the coffee. She was tall and slim and very pretty with dark auburn hair and a dusting of freckles on her nose.

"Where are you from Laura?"

"I was raised in Greeley so Ft. Collins is pretty close to my home and my family."

"Oh, are you graduating this year too?"

"No, I've got two more years to go. I'm going to be a teacher, hopefully. Charles tells me you were, I mean are, a teacher too. I'm sure you have some wonderful stories about your years teaching. I understand that you taught in a one-room school house and had all eight grades. That must have been very challenging."

"Yes, it was a challenge, but I only taught for one year. Frank, Charles' father rescued me from myself and I've been a farmer's wife forever it seems. So, may I ask, how long have you and Charlie been "friends"?"

"We've known each other for a year or so, and started dating just before summer vacation. We've been writing to each other over the summer and we reconnected when we came back to school a month or so ago."

Elizabeth thought to herself, "So that's why he made such a big deal about picking up the mail. It all makes sense now."

"What are you two talking about in here? Do I smell coffee? I'd love some coffee, how about you Dad?"

"Yes, that sounds great, a cup of coffee's just what the doctor ordered. Elizabeth did we bring anything to eat? I'm starved!"

"Of course – I completely forgot! Charles can you get the picnic basket out of the back seat of the car? I brought some fried chicken and potato salad and of course your favorite apple pie."

"I didn't know you liked apple pie. That's good to know." Laura smiled at Charles over her shoulder as she poured the coffee.

After their lunch Laura excused herself, saying she had to get back to the dorm. She said she would see them again before they left, gave Charles a kiss on the cheek, hugged Frank and Elizabeth and left them standing in the kitchen.

"Well, what do you think?"

"What do we think about what?" Frank teased.

"Laura! I think she's just about the most perfect person in the world and I want to marry her, if her parents approve. Oh, and if you both approve as well, of course." He was nervous but excited.

"Isn't this kind of sudden?" Elizabeth asked.

"Not really Mom. I've known her for over a year and we started dating seriously last spring."

"That's what Laura said."

"What? did you already ask her? You don't waste any time do you? Was she okay with all the questions?"

"Well, I didn't ask her a lot of questions. I just wanted to know a little bit about her and about how serious you two are. It looks like you're pretty serious."

Frank interrupted "Charles when are you thinking of getting married? Do you have a set plan for your future? You know supporting a wife and family is not an easy thing. It's not something you should do without a lot of careful consideration and planning." He didn't believe in beating around the bush.

"I've given this a lot of thought. I saved enough money over the past three summers to put a down payment on a place and I found one just a few miles from you. Do you remember the Christianson place? Well, Mr. Christianson passed away over a year ago. It's been vacant for quite a while but the house and outbuildings are in pretty good shape and they're anxious to sell. Of course, the house will need some repair, but I've spent enough time watching you that I think I can fix most of the things, if you'll help me of course."

"Yes, I know the Christianson place. Mr. Christianson was a fine man and a good farmer. It's a nice place and a good piece of farm land too. But, do you have enough money to buy a tractor and farming equipment too? When I started out, I was lucky to get my land for free by just improving it. Things are a lot different now. It costs a lot to get started in the farming business."

"I realize that. I've been talking with the school board in Hartford and I think they're going to offer me a job teaching at the high school next year. That income will help me get by. Laura is studying to be a teacher and I think she should be able to get a job there too. So we'll have two incomes for a while any way."

"You have been thinking about this haven't you? I'm proud of you son. Well, if there's anything your mother and I can do to help get you started you know we will. I can even bring my tractor and equipment over next spring and we can get a crop planted."

"Charles, have you asked Laura to marry you? Does she know about your plans?"

"Yes, I asked her as soon as I got back to Ft. Collins. She said yes and we've been talking about our future non-stop. I met her parents last spring and I liked them and believe it or not, they liked me too!" He was blushing. "I hate to spring this on you, but they're coming here to Ft. Collins tomorrow to meet you. Laura and I were planning to have a nice dinner for the six of us so you could all get to know one another. What do you think? Can you stay an extra day?"

"I'm sure we can stay an extra day. I would like to meet her parents and spend a little more time with her. After all, you're our oldest and we want the best for you."

"I know that Mom, and I think I've found her."

They met Laura's family the next day and were impressed. Her father owned a pharmacy and her mother and Elizabeth had a lot in common. The families promised to keep in touch about making plans for a wedding the following spring.

They drove home in silence - they were each in their own world thinking about their son's future. Their family was changing before their eyes.

Chapter

# NINETEEN

Mary and Margaret had graduated from high school, and they each had their own plan for the future.

Mary agreed to go to the Normal School in Denver that Elizabeth had attended. This was a temporary detour in her plan to go to Hollywood. Frank and Elizabeth insisted that she get some sort of education in case stardom wasn't everything she'd hoped it would be. That put her plans on hold for two years, but she was a very determined young woman. She had become a cheerleader, of course, and was voted class president as well. She was impatient to get on with her "real life" as she called it, but accepted the fact that she might have to support herself for a while, just until she became a "star". She lived with Lois and Jacob while she went to school.

Margaret was accepted by the University of Denver's School of Music. She had sent them her application and was asked to attend an audition in September. They were impressed with her musical ability and offered her a full scholarship. She had been a member of the high school marching band and had learned to play the French horn expertly. She was first chair by the time she was a junior in high school in the concert band as well. She loved music and planned to become a professional musician some day. Her ambition was to live in New York City and play at Carnegie Hall. Frank and Elizabeth were supportive of her dreams, but really didn't want her to live so far away.

They decided to make a trip to New York so Maggie could see what the big city was really like That way they could see it too. Neither of them had been even close to New York and the thought was intimidating. They managed to get a hired hand to stay at the farm and they all went "back east" at Thanksgiving.

The city was everything they thought it would be – crowded, loud, and expensive. And everything Maggie hoped it would be – beautiful, exciting and wonderful! "Well, if this is what she has her heart set on… At least we have a few years before we really have to worry about it." They told each other.

Thank goodness Emily and Joseph were still young enough that they wouldn't have to worry about them leaving for several years. Emily was "twelve going on twenty", and Joe was ten. They were good kids and their adolescent problems were much easier to deal with than the issues of their older siblings.

# TWENTY

Their lives continued on as usual – there were ups and downs along the way of course, but Frank and Elizabeth were still very much in love.

Charles graduated and just like he planned, he bought the Christianson place. He and Laura married and moved on to the farm – now called the "Young Wagner Place" – and began their lives together. At first Frank helped Charles farm the land and Elizabeth helped Laura set up their household, but very soon they were on their own and were doing very well. Charles and Laura both taught at the high school in town until they saved enough money so that Charles could farm full-time.

Within just a few years they were seeing a nice profit from the modern farming methods that Charles had learned in college. They had been married four years when they announced that they were going to add a new member to their family.

Elizabeth and Frank were ecstatic! They were going to be grandparents! This was the best news yet! Elizabeth started knitting baby things right away and of course Frank was already talking about making a rocking horse or a doll bed, depending on who this new little person might be.

"Frank, do I look like a grandmother to you?' she asked. "I

certainly don't feel old enough to be a grandmother." She sat at her dressing table surveying herself in the mirror.

He was sitting on the edge of the bed putting his socks on, "well, you DO have white hair, but I'm used to that and you don't have too many wrinkles, so no you don't look old enough to be a grandmother. At least not to me."

She laughed, "You always tell it like it is don't you?" "Maybe I should dye my hair, what do you think?"

"I think that would be silly, after all you're 50 years old and most women that age are starting to get gray hair. Plus, I can't see you fussing around dying and re-dying your hair for the rest of your life. Just leave it alone – you look perfect to me." He leaned over her shoulder and looked at her in the mirror. "But, if you want to dye your hair, go ahead – but dye it red. I've always liked redheads. Anyway, I know you'll do whatever you want to in the end." He winked at her and gave her a kiss on the neck. "I'm going to milk, see you in bit. I'd really like some biscuits and gravy this morning."

She called after him, "Redheads?? When did you start liking redheads?? Oh, and by the way I'm only 49 years old!" "Have Joe help you. I think I heard him up and around in his room." School hadn't started yet so he and Emily were still living on the ranch. They were both in high school and just like their older brother and sisters they boarded in town during the school year.

"I don't really need him to help me with the milking, I've got some other chores I want him to do before he leaves. But I am going to get the princess up. She needs to help a little more around here."

He was right. Emily was off in her own little world most of the time. She wanted to be an architect some day and spent hours drawing buildings and floor plans. She still loved numbers and how they worked in her designs.

Over breakfast Frank told Joe he needed him to help with the cattle. He was going to bring the heifers in from the pasture so they could check them over and vaccinate them. Later they would drive the steers in and get them ready to be shipped to the rail yards to sell.

Frank thought Joe would make a fine veterinarian one day. He had a natural way with the animals and liked taking care of them and making sure they were healthy. He was calm and didn't get rattled when a cow had complications giving birth or a horse got injured and the livestock responded well to him when he took care of them.

"It sure is a lot easier to get them into town in a truck than the way we used to do it." Frank remembered the times when he and his neighbors drove their cattle to town using horses and dogs. It was a nerve-wracking experience making sure none of the cattle got hurt or ran away. Their livelihoods depended on the sale of their herds.

"Yeah, but not nearly as much fun, I'll bet." They had gotten him a nice buckskin gelding to ride and he spent hours in the pastures on horseback checking for new calves or fixing fences, or just enjoying his life. He didn't like school very much and wasn't looking forward to living in town for the next few months.

They were just cleaning up the dishes when Lucy started to bark her "somebody's here" bark. Frank looked out the kitchen window just as a pickup truck and a horse trailer pulled into the yard. "Who the heck is this?" he thought. He watched as a man wearing a big cowboy hat got out of the driver's seat and went around and opened the passenger's door. A woman got out of the pickup - it was Mary and she had a cast on her leg. "Elizabeth! It's Mary - Mary's home!"

They ran outside to greet Mary and the man. "Mary, Honey!! It's so good to see you! How are you? Oh my, what happened to your leg?" They all talked at once, clambering for her attention. She looked tired and drawn, as if her leg was very painful. As they helped her into the house she said "This is my friend George Dawson. We just finished shooting a movie up in Wyoming and thought we'd come and visit my family for a few days I hope you don't mind."

"Mind? Of course, we don't mind. George, I'm Mary's father Frank Wagner". He extended his hand to the stranger. "Thank you for bringing our daughter home. Do you want to take the horses out of the trailer?"

George shook Frank's hand, "It's nice to meet you sir, I've heard a lot about Mary's family. Yes, the horses have had a long trip and need some feed and water."

"This is my wife Elizabeth and our daughter Emily and son Joseph. Joe, can you help Mr. Dawson with the horses? Come on in and have something to eat when you get them settled."

Elizabeth helped Mary into a chair and brought her a cup of coffee. "My goodness Mary, when did you break your leg?"

"It happened a couple of days ago. We were shooting a Western near Laramie and the horse I was riding stumbled and fell and landed on my right leg. The company doctor patched me up but I won't be able to work for several weeks, maybe even months."

She'd been working as a stunt rider for several years in Hollywood and had appeared in several moving pictures. The family had seen her perform whenever one of her movies came to town. She always let them know which movie she was in and what she was wearing so they could pick her out. She hadn't been interested in any speaking parts.

Emily and Joe were enthralled with their movie star sister, but Elizabeth and Frank worried about her. It looked like a dangerous profession to them.

"Mary, who's this George fellow? Is he a stunt rider too?"

"No Mother, George is a "wrangler", he takes care of the livestock and travels with the movie crew. He has a ranch in Montana, outside of Helena where he runs cattle and a few horses on open range. He's going back there now that we've wrapped up this latest picture."

"Well, you can stay here for as long as you want to. We're so happy to see you and know that you're alright – for the most part."

"Honestly, I'm afraid that this time I won't be able to bounce back like I have in the past. The doctor said that I broke my femur. George wants me to go to Montana with him but I can't travel for awhile, it's too painful."

"Does George want to marry you?"

"Oh Mom, this is 1934, don't be so old-fashioned. I'm pretty sure he does but I'm not sure I want to get married, at least not right away. I like my independence and don't want a man telling me what to do or where to be."

Elizabeth didn't know what to say. She knew that Mary was rebellious, but she didn't like the fact that she was willing to live with a man even though it was 1934. She was worried about how Frank was going to take the news.

Frank, George and Joe came in the house, talking like old friends. "Elizabeth, can you feed this man? He looks like he could use a good meal. Mary, how's your leg? Are you able to walk on it at all?"

Elizabeth went into the kitchen with Emily to make something for Mary and George. Emily was all starry-eyed and obviously thought George was some sort of movie star.

It was decided that Mary would stay with her family for a few weeks and that George would go home to Montana. He offered to take her horses with him, but she declined, saying she wanted to keep them and work with them while she recuperated. She told him she'd let him know when she was able to work again. She really just didn't want any encumbrances. The director of the movie company sent her a letter along with her last paycheck. The letter said that she could work for them again, if and when she was fully recovered, but they would have to be sure she was able to do her job. That didn't sound very promising.

Soon, she was up and around and able to ride, with a little help getting in the saddle. She realized that her stunt riding days were numbered and was carefully weighing her options. Should she go to Montana and marry George, or try to get a job teaching school here in Colorado? At this point she was happy that her parents had insisted that she get her teaching certificate. She was just 23, and still had her whole life ahead of her. Then, one morning Elizabeth watched as a cloud of dust neared their lane. It was George's pickup and horse trailer. It seemed that Mary had made her decision.

Charles and Laura stood with the couple while the Justice of the

Peace married them a few days later. Elizabeth gave a huge sigh of relief. At least they were properly and legally married…..

"She'll do fine up there in Montana on a ranch. George said there's an opening for a teacher at the school in town, so she'll still be independent if she wants to be." Frank had his arm around Elizabeth's shoulder as they watched them drive away. "She loves the outdoors and she'll make George a good wife once she settles down and realizes that she's not always right. A marriage takes a lot of give and take, but mostly give."

"Is that right? Do you think you've given more than you've taken over the years Frank Wagner?"

"No, I think YOU'VE given more than you've taken and I've just been along for the ride! Now let's have some of that wedding cake you made, if there's any left." He patted her on the behind as they went into the house.

# TWENTY-ONE

Margaret sat in her little flat writing her weekly letter to her parents. It was another tale of fiction and fantasy. She just couldn't tell them the truth. Her letters detailed successful auditions and performances with standing ovations. Nothing could have been farther from the truth. Yes, she had a lovely singing voice and could play the piano splendidly, but there were at least thirty other women who were just as good and five who were much better. She was hired as an understudy in an off-Broadway show that closed in just one week. She tried to find work giving piano and singing lessons, but didn't have her own piano or a place to teach. She had a couple of students who lived in her neighborhood, but she wasn't making enough money to support herself.

As she waited outside the director's office for one more audition, she noticed a young man sitting on a bench across from her. He was holding a violin case and was obviously auditioning as well. He was tall and thin and very handsome in a dark, exotic way. After the audition she walked down the stairs to the street, knowing that she hadn't gotten the job. When she opened the door, the young man was there waiting for her.

"Hello! My name is Benjamin Stein and I couldn't help but notice you upstairs. How did your audition go?"

"Hello, Mr. Stein, I'm Margaret Wagner and I don't think my audition was very successful. What about you – do you think you did well?"

"I'm not sure, but probably not. Would you like a cup of tea – my grandmother always says 'a little tea goes well with a little sympathy'".

"I'd love a cup of tea, and I think your grandmother sounds very smart, but I don't go with men I haven't been properly introduced to."

"Oh, I see. Wait right here – I'll be right back."

She watched him run down the street and soon saw that he was coming back with another young man who looked a lot like him.

The other young man said, "Miss Wagner, may I present my brother Benjamin Stein? He's an upstanding young man and is completely harmless, honest!"

She couldn't help but laugh. "This is a proper introduction? Well, I am impressed with your ingenuity Mr. Stein, so yes I will have a cup of tea with you, with or without the sympathy."

They spent an enjoyable hour getting to know each other. She told him she was from Colorado, had studied music in Denver and was becoming more and more disillusioned with New York.

He said he'd never met anyone from "out west" but was interested in learning everything about it. Were there really Indians roaming the streets and was the Grand Canyon as enormous as he'd heard.

She laughed, "No there aren't any aborigines wandering around Denver. It's really a rather sophisticated city and the Grand Canyon is in Arizona, not even close to Colorado."

"I thought the Colorado River ran through the Grand Canyon – am I wrong?"

"No, you're right about that but the Grand Canyon is NOT in Colorado. So, tell me about you, all I know is that you're from 'back east'".

"Okay, where do I start? My family is Jewish – have you ever met a Jew? My brother and I live with our parents. My father works in the "Garment District" selling ladies clothes. I started playing the violin at age six and someday hope to make a living as a musician. My brother is going to be a lawyer but right now he's still an undergraduate at NYU. Is there anything else you'd like to know? Oh, and I'm single and available and think you are absolutely beautiful!"

She blushed at that. He was very glib and sure of himself, she thought. She hadn't had a lot of experience with men, especially New Yorkers and she felt overwhelmed by his big personality.

"Where do you live, Miss Wagner? May I walk you home?"

"No thank you Mr. Stein, I can find my way home just fine. It's been nice talking with you and thank you for the tea. Good day."

He must have followed her because the next day when she went out for another audition he was waiting on her corner. "Hello Miss Wagner! I was hoping I'd run into you!"

"I don't think we ran into each other Mr. Stein – I think you've been waiting for me."

"You're right, I have been waiting for you and I would like to wait for you for the rest of my life!"

"Was he serious?" she thought. "Mr. Stein I hope you really are harmless, because you're scaring me."

"I'm truly sorry Miss Wagner. I have a tendency to be a little dramatic. Honestly, I do find you very attractive and would like nothing better than to get to know you. And I really am harmless, I promise."

Ben and Margaret eventually both got positions in an orchestra where they saw each other every day. Finally, Margaret was able to write her parents with truly good news and felt much better about her decision to come to New York.

They began seeing each other regularly and found they had a lot in common. One day Ben asked her to come to his house for dinner he wanted to introduce her to the rest of his family.

She suggested the following Saturday. "I'm sorry, Maggie, but that's our Sabbath and we don't entertain on that evening."

"Oh, would Sunday work?" She realized that she knew nothing about his religion.

"Absolutely! I'll let my mother know. She'll want to make a special dinner to impress you!"

Margaret liked his father immediately, but his mother was another story. She looked Margaret up and down and muttered something about her "being a skinny Gentile". The dinner was delicious and Margaret made a point of complimenting Mrs. Stein and asking for her recipe for the baked chicken.

Ben walked Margaret home and said he just knew his mother loved her and they would be good friends one day. Margaret wasn't so sure.

When he got home his mother was waiting for him. "What are you thinking bringing that girl to my home? I can see why you are interested in her, but Benjie she's not one of us!"

His father spoke up, "Now Ruth, there is nothing wrong with that girl. She was wearing very nice clothes and she has wonderful manners. Ben could do much worse." He had no idea that those "very nice clothes" were hand made with love by her mother.

Margaret wrote her parents and told them about her new job and her new friend. Elizabeth thought, "This is what I was afraid of. I hope she doesn't marry some complete stranger and never come back home. I wonder if this Benjamin character is a good man or one of those city slickers."

Frank was more pragmatic, "Margaret has a good head on her shoulders. She's not going to take up with just anyone. Have a little faith, Elizabeth. After all, she is your daughter and is an awful lot like you were at that age."

And so, their relationship continued to blossom and despite their cultural differences Margaret and Benjamin fell in love and got married. They were married at the courthouse in New York City. Frank and Elizabeth made the long trip to New York for the wedding and felt that Ben was a fine young man who obviously adored their daughter. Ben's family all seemed to truly care for Margaret, even his mother, and they went back to the farm feeling satisfied with Margaret's choices – in life and in love.

# TWENTY-TWO

It was late August, 1935 and the weather was hot. The temperatures had been in the nineties for days and it hadn't rained for weeks. The harvesters had come and gone. There hadn't been much for them to harvest, the crops weren't very good this year. The cattle weren't as fat as usual, the pastures were sparse and they had to work hard to get enough to eat. Frank was worried. Elizabeth would find him standing in the yard looking into the distance – willing the clouds to build and bring rain.

Joseph had entered a steer in the county fair and the whole family was in town to watch the judging and to enjoy the festivities. Frank, Elizabeth and Emily were sitting in the grand stands watching the rodeo. Joe was in the exhibitors' barn with his steer when one of their neighbors came and sat beside Frank.

Frank said, "What?!? When did this happen? Elizabeth, Emily we have to get home right away."

"What's wrong? What's happened?"

"Melvin just told me that our cattle got into his cane field. You know, he never maintains his fences, and they ate the whole crop."

"Cane? Won't that make them sick if they eat too much?"

"Yes, especially if they get to the water trough and drink too much water. They can only digest small amounts of cane and the water makes it even worse. We need to get home as soon as we can. Emily, go tell your brother we're leaving. Hopefully he can get a ride home or maybe just stay in the barn with his steer until we can come and get him."

When they pulled into the yard they were appalled by what they saw. There were at least twenty of their cows lying on their sides, their bellies were swollen and distended and they were obviously in pain. "Oh my god Frank, what can we do for them? Are they dying?"

"I'm afraid there's nothing we can do and none of them are going to live. We have to make sure none of the others get to the water." He had tears in his eyes. Elizabeth had never seen him look so defeated. These cattle were their livelihood, especially with the poor wheat and corn crops.

Emily ran to close the gate, "Daddy, there are more cattle out here in the lane. It looks like they drank the water and then tried to go back to the pasture."

After they counted the animals they found that they had lost over half of their herd and both bulls were dead.

"I just don't know what we're going to do now. This is more than we can handle I'm afraid."

They spent the next few days moving the bodies out to the far pasture and burning their carcasses. The smoke could be seen for miles. The saying was true – their whole world had gone up in smoke.

Elizabeth held her husband's head against her breast. He was close to tears, "I'm not a quitter, but I do know when I've been beaten. I don't know how we can recover from this set back."

"I've been thinking Frank – we've still got almost half of our cattle and the milk cows and I've got my chickens. We can sell cream and eggs. We'll have to tighten our belts and make some changes to our lives, but we can get through this together." They called Emily and Joe to the kitchen the next morning and told them about their plan.

"If there's anything we can do to help just tell us. I don't have to go to college next year. That will save a lot of money. Maybe I can get a job in town at the mercantile or for the newspaper. Joe, I'm sure you can find some work to do too."

"Emily that's wonderful of you, but we have money set aside for your education and with your grades I'm pretty sure you can get a scholarship like Margaret did. We don't want you to make that big of a sacrifice if you don't have to."

Joe said, "I'm going to get a good price for my steer, so I'll give that money to the family fund."

"No Joseph, you put that money in your savings account. You're going to need it in a couple of years to go to college too. We'll make out just fine. We have each other and this is not going to beat us."

Charles and Laura helped them as much as they could. Their crops weren't very good but they still had a good herd of cattle and they had a bull that Frank and Elizabeth could borrow.

The next couple of years weren't easy, but they still had their faith in God and each other. Eventually they were able to rebuild their lives. Ultimately, they were more appreciative of what they had and didn't take their good fortune for granted as they had done in the past.

# TWENTY-THREE

It was 1940 and Emily was graduating from the University of Colorado's Architectural school. She skipped a grade in elementary school so she was barely 23. She had gotten a scholarship that paid for her tuition and books and she worked part-time to help pay for her living expenses. She was one of the few women in the program. She loved every minute of her time in college and hated to see it come to an end. Her father was her biggest fan, he understood the skill it took to take a blank sheet of paper and turn an idea into an actual building. Her designs were artistic and creative, yet functional and she earned a reputation as being one of the best in her class. She was offered an apprenticeship with a good firm in Boulder. Her plan was to work for them for three years, then apply for her architectural license and open her own office.

Frank, Elizabeth and Joe were at the graduation ceremony along with Charles and Laura and their two children, James and Amanda. (Charles had named his son after his little brother). They were all so proud of Emily. It was a difficult curriculum and took an additional two years of college after she received her under-graduate degree. They were all sure that she would achieve her dream.

When they arrived in Boulder for the graduation Elizabeth was surprised to see that Emily had cut her long hair. She had always worn it in a braid or a bun, but now it was shoulder-length and she looked very modern. Elizabeth felt as thought she could see Emily's future opening up in front of her and her daughter was ready to cross the threshold to meet it head on with determination and courage. That is, if the world would allow her to.

There was a war going on in Europe and there were rumblings that the U.S. was going to get involved. No one knew how that would affect them, they would just have to take a wait and see attitude and hope for the best.

The war in Europe had repercussions all across the U.S. It was difficult to get building supplies and most construction had come to a complete halt. In her new job, Emily was more of a secretary than an architect-in-training. The firm she worked for didn't have any architectural work for her to do, but were willing to keep her employed. She was just happy to have an income. She spent her spare time looking at blueprints and asking questions so she was learning.

"Emily, what are you doing on Sunday?" She and Yvonne Schwartz the company receptionist, were eating their sack lunches in the break room.

"My brother Joe's coming down this Sunday. There's a really good Italian restaurant we both like and we're going to splurge. Why?"

"Oh, I just thought if you weren't busy you'd like to get together."

"Why don't you come too? Do you like Italian food? If you do, you'll love this place!"

"I love Italian, so, yes I'd like to come with you, but the real reason I asked what you were doing is that I want you to meet my brother Roger."

Emily started to say something.

"Wait, don't look so skeptical, he's really nice and I think the two of you would be perfect together!! Please, just this once. He's really nice – I promise!"

When Joseph came to her apartment to pick her up she told him about the slight change in plans.

"I guess its okay, the "more the merrier" but I hope they won't expect me to pay for their dinners. Dr. Wickes doesn't pay me that much to help him in his vet clinic."

"Oh, you Scrooge! I'll make sure we get separate checks. We'll go "Dutch". She laughed and poked him in the ribs. "Let's go, I told them we'd be there at 6 and it's already 5:30."

They had a great time, sharing stories about their siblings and getting to know one another. After dinner they all went to Emily's and played cards and laughed some more.

"Its 11:00, I'd better get going. I've got a long drive ahead of me and an early class tomorrow morning. It was nice to meet both of you, hope to see you again."

"Wow I had no idea it was that late. Yes, we'd better get out of here too, Yvonne. Thank you for a lovely evening Emily, I hope we can do it again some time."

"I would like that Roger, it was fun. See you tomorrow Yvonne."

She realized that she hadn't laughed that much for a very long time. She liked Roger, a lot!

Soon, the four of them were getting together every week. Joe made the drive down to Denver or Roger would drive the girls up to Ft. Collins. Sometimes they'd meet halfway in Greeley. Yvonne was right, Roger was really nice and Joe liked him too. Emily looked forward to their Sundays.

One evening as she walked home from work, she saw Roger's car. He pulled over and leaned over to the passenger side. "Hello Miss, can I give you a lift?"

"Sorry sir, I don't take rides from strangers." She laughed.

"Come on, hop in. I'll take you anywhere you want to go. Let's just get you out of the cold."

"It is cold. Okay, let's go to that little coffee shop on Colfax."

"That sounds great, here let me get the door for you." He jumped out and opened her door.

They sat in the coffee shop drinking coffee and getting warm, "Emily I hope you don't mind. I just wanted to spend some time with just you, without Yvonne and Joe. We always have fun together, but I'd like to get to know you better."

And so, Emily and Roger began dating.

# TWENTY-FIVE

Frank and Elizabeth traveled to Denver for Thanksgiving. Frank was going to spend some time with Joseph and Elizabeth was going to go shopping with Emily, then they were going to trade places. She would go to Ft. Collins and Frank would stay with Emily.

"Emily, we need to go to the grocery store. You don't have anything in this house to cook with."

"I know Mom, I don't cook many turkey dinners. I usually just make a sandwich for myself."

"That's pretty obvious. Get your coat, you can show me how to get to the store. Frank, Emily and I are going to get supplies for tomorrow."

"I'll just wait here, it's nice to be able to listen to the radio and not have to worry about it dying on me." He'd hooked a wind generator up to the windmill that provided electricity to the farm house. The only problem was that if there wasn't enough wind, there wasn't enough power for the lights and the radio at the same time. They'd be right in the middle of a radio program when the batteries would die and the power would go out. Luckily the wind blew most of the time so they could listen to the radio for about an hour at a time.

Elizabeth drove their car, "Denver has sure changed since I lived here."

"That's right – I forgot that you used to live in Denver. Where did you live?"

"Your grandparents, Aunt Lois and I lived just a few blocks from here. Let's take a little drive and I'll show you where we lived. My father had a tailor business and we lived in the apartment above the shop. Did you remember that I went to college here too?"

"Yes I remembered that, because Mary went to the same school, didn't she?"

"She did. I loved living here, but I've gotten used to the slower pace and quiet of country life."

They spent an hour driving around the Denver area, with Elizabeth pointing out landmarks to Emily and remarking on how things had changed. Emily didn't have a car so most of this was new to her.

They were in a nice, big grocery store that had everything they would need for their dinner. "Mother, how big of a turkey do you think we should get?"

"Not too big, there are only the four of us, and that's a good thing - your oven is pretty small. By the way does it work? Have you ever used it?"

"Yes it works I baked a cake once. But, there will be six of us. I've asked my friend Yvonne from work and her brother Roger to come for dinner too." She looked at the toes of her shoes.

Elizabeth noticed that her daughter was blushing, "Yvonne and Roger? Is there anything I should know? You look like the cat that ate the cream." She lifted Emily's chin up and looked at her face. "This Roger fellow, he's important to you isn't he? Well, I can't wait to meet him and to tell your father."

"Mother! Don't say anything to Daddy yet. We're just friends."

"Oh, I see, "just friends". Okay, but I'm looking forward to meeting your "friend". Well, I'm glad you told me, we certainly don't want to run out of food the first time we meet your "friend". Relax,

Honey, we won't embarrass you – intentionally!" She laughed and gave her daughter a hug and together they finished their shopping.

Later that night as they got into Emily's bed, Elizabeth said "We're going to have guests for dinner tomorrow. Emily's friend Yvonne and her brother Roger are coming. I think there's something special about this Roger person, Emily lights up like a Christmas tree when she talks about him."

"What?? I didn't know she had a beau! How long has this been going on?"

"Sshh, she'll hear you, she's just in the other room on the couch, you know. I'm not sure how long they've been seeing each other, maybe we can ask Joe. At least we'll be able to meet him before she decides to marry the man, not like Maggie."

The dinner was a success. Elizabeth and Frank were surprised to see that the four young people were such good friends. They all seemed to genuinely like each other. But most importantly, they liked Roger. As they got ready for bed Frank said, "This Roger has a good head on his shoulders. He seems to have his future planned out."

"I like the way he treats his sister. You can always tell how a man will treat his wife by the way he treats his mother or sister. And he certainly likes our daughter. They make a nice couple, don't you think?"

"Let's not get too carried away, after all she says they're just friends."

Joe stayed at Emily's and the next day entertained them with stories about the vet clinic where he worked. In the meantime, Emily and Frank talked about the new things she'd learned at the architectural office. Both of their children seemed to have found their niche and were happily looking to the future. Frank and Elizabeth made the trip home in a contented silence. Their kids were all growing up and getting settled in their lives.

Emily and Roger and Yvonne and Joe met nearly every weekend. One Sunday afternoon in December of 1941 the two young couples went to the movies together. While they were watching the movie there was an announcement – the Japanese had bombed Pearl Harbor. The young people were shocked and as they left the theater, both men decided to enlist in the military. First thing Monday morning, Roger enlisted in the Army and Joseph went to the Navy recruiter's office.

Joseph and Emily went home to visit their parents so Joseph could tell them about his decision to enlist. Frank and Elizabeth were upset and worried about their son to say the least, but realized that there was nothing they could do or say to change his mind. They were aware of the problems in the world and had gotten letters from Margaret telling them about the terrible things that were happening to the Jews in Eastern Europe. Several of Benjamin's relatives had lost their homes and businesses to the Germans and some had been arrested for unspecified crimes. Neither Frank nor Elizabeth had experienced a war, but knew that this was going to change all of their lives forever.

They left Hartford with their parents' blessings but Elizabeth couldn't hide her tears. When they got back to Denver, Joseph was given a series of tests at the Navy recruiter's office. He scored very well, so he was sent to the Naval Academy in Annapolis, Maryland. He would be there for two years and then would most likely be shipped to the Pacific. He was going to be part of a special, war-time program that sped up the training process and enabled young men with potential to become junior officers in much less time than the traditional system.

Emily stood on her tiptoes to give her brother a kiss on the cheek and a big hug. "Take care of yourself little brother. Be careful, okay?"

"I will sis. You take care too, and take care of Yvonne for me, will you?"

She watched the train leave Denver with a deep sense of loss. She and Joe had always been very close. Roger and Yvonne had gone with them to the station. Yvonne was crying inconsolably while Emily tried to be strong. Obviously, her brother and Yvonne had become more than just friends.

She and Roger had been dating steadily for several months. He would be leaving within a few weeks and after basic training, he was going directly to England. Roger's parents were originally from Germany and he spoke German fluently. He was a good candidate to work in an Intelligence unit and translate coded messages that were intercepted from the war front.

"I know I don't have the right to ask you, but will you wait for me? I don't know how long this war will last, but I love you and hope that we can be together forever when it's over."

"I love you too Roger, and of course I'll wait for you, no matter how long it takes."

She and Yvonne were good friends but, with Roger and Joe both gone, Emily was lost. The building industry was at a standstill and she wanted to do something important with her life and for her country. Roger wrote regularly and told her all about the English countryside and how much he missed her. He told her that someone with her ability would be very valuable to the war effort. She had always loved numbers, languages and puzzles. Roger thought she would be great working as a cryptographer decoding messages from the Germans. He would translate them and she would decode them. They both agreed that it sounded like a perfect fit for her.

Soon she was on her way back from Hartford with her parents' okay, if not their blessing, to enlist in the WAC's. She was accepted and within a few weeks found herself on a plane to London where Roger was anxiously awaiting her arrival. Roger and Emily worked together for two years and they eventually married.

# TWENTY-SIX

Joseph spent his two years at the Naval Academy. His letters to his parents spoke of how badly the people of Annapolis treated the sailors. He told them about the signs in yards everywhere that said "Sailors and Dogs Keep Off the Grass!" The people who lived there didn't like the seamen at all. He wrote to tell them that he would be home for a couple of weeks before shipping out. When Elizabeth, Frank and Charles and his family met him at the train station they barely recognized him. He seemed to have grown a foot and had put on a lot of weight. He looked handsome in his dress uniform.

Elizabeth's eyes filled with tears, "Joe you look wonderful! Military life seems to suit you. Here, let me take a good look at you!"

"Thanks Mom, but I can't wait to sleep in my own bedroom and eat some of your home cooking. I've told all my buddies about your biscuits and gravy." He bent down and kissed her cheek.

Frank embraced his son. "I'm glad you were able to spend some time with us before you go to sea. When do you ship out and do you know what ship you'll be assigned to?"

Charles grabbed his younger brother in a big bear hug. "Hey little brother you look pretty sharp in that blue suit! Are you pretending to be a fireman?"

"Charles, give me a chance to get my hug from your little brother.

Joe, Charlie's just jealous because his overalls don't have those pretty gold buttons!" Laura gave Joe a big hug too as Amanda and James shyly looked at their uncle.

"Is that Amanda? Gosh you've become quite a young lady! I'll bet you've got a lot of beaus. And James you're almost as tall as your mother! Has it been that long since I've been home?"

"Uncle Joe! I don't have any beaus! Jimmy, don't say a word or else!"

James laughed at his little sister. "Sure, you don't have any boy friends - that's rich! What about …"

She chased him, "I warned you Jimmy!"

The adults all laughed. "Let's get this sailor home and get some food into him. Charles, you and Laura are coming aren't you?"

"We wouldn't miss it. We'll be there as soon as we get the chores done. Come on kids, let's go home! Mother Wagner, I'll bring a pie. I know Joseph likes apple pie."

"That sounds good Laura, we'll see you in a little while."

As they drove home Joe told them that he would be staying for about ten days. He had to be in Los Angeles to ship out in three weeks. "I don't know which ship I'll be on, but as soon as I find out I'll let you know. I want to stop in Denver and see Yvonne before I go."

Frank and Elizabeth shared a knowing look and smiled. "She's a nice girl Joe. Emily certainly likes her brother, so there must be some family attraction there." Frank grinned at his son.

The days went by too fast and before they knew it, they were taking their youngest son to the train station. He was going into harm's way and there was nothing they could do to protect him. Elizabeth tried not to cry, but as the train pulled away the tears ran down her cheeks. "We've still got each other Elizabeth. Now we just have to pray that all of our children stay safe." He put his arms around her and held her close to his heart.

# TWENTY-SEVEN

Joseph was stationed on the USS Wichita, a heavy cruiser. They immediately sailed for the South Pacific. The ship was part of a fleet including destroyers, troop carriers and battleships. They were involved in the attack on Okinawa and were hit by a Japanese torpedo and several "kamikaze" air strikes. Their main responsibility was to provide air support while the battleships bombed their assigned targets. Joe witnessed and experienced many things that affected him for the rest of his life. One of the worst things was when he and the rest of the crew were assigned the task of freeing a prisoner of war camp on Nagasaki. The things he saw would haunt him forever.

Joe was merely a Lieutenant JG (Junior Grade) but he was an officer and as such he was present when Emperor Hirohito surrendered to the United States on the battleship USS Missouri. His ship was part of the fleet that accompanied the Missouri. This was one of the most memorable moments of his life.

Meanwhile, the folks back home were dealing with rationing and the worries of a major war. Frank and Elizabeth were rationed on the amount of sugar, flour, coffee, or tea they were allowed to buy. They used ration cards and were careful not to waste anything. The American people were limited to the amount of gasoline they could use and this curtailed most travel. Farmers, however, were allowed enough diesel fuel to enable them to raise their crops and feed the country. The people were more than willing to tighten their belts if it helped the war effort.

Frank and Elizabeth had volunteered to become members of the Colorado Civil Air Patrol, which sounded a lot more important than it actually was. They were supposed to monitor airplane activity over their farm. When they would hear an airplane they would grab binoculars and try to see what type of plane was flying over. They had a template showing the types of planes. They would enter the date and make a note on a chart they had been provided showing the activity in the skies over Colorado. They kept a journal of these sightings and once a month they would meet with other people in the county and give their information to the CAP. It was just something to help them feel that they were doing their part.

Elizabeth worried constantly about her son and daughter. She was unable to sleep and spent many a night reading until the sun came up. It helped keep her mind off the danger Joe and Emily might be in.

Frank came into the kitchen where Elizabeth was drinking a cup of chicory and warm milk. "You're up early or are you still up? Couldn't sleep?" Frank was exhausted after each day, and fell asleep as soon as his head hit the pillow. His work load had gotten heavier with each passing year. "I'm thinking about hiring one of the Sherman boys to give me a hand in the fields this year. It takes me so long to get anything done and I'm so "dog-tired" that it just might be worth the expense."

He looked tired and he'd aged in the last couple of years. His hair was almost as white as Elizabeth's. "Of course. you should get help if you can. But I heard that the Sherman boys have both enlisted in the army and are leaving in a few weeks. Maybe you could get Charlie to give you a hand, or Jim. He's getting to be a big boy. I'm sure he'd like to earn a little spending money."

"That's not a bad idea. I'll ask Charlie if he can spare the boy. That would be a plus for everyone. You always come up with a solution, don't you?" He gave her hand a squeeze as he went outside to milk the cows.

Charles agreed to let James help Frank and he started working after school and on weekends. It took a lot of the burden off of Frank and Elizabeth was grateful. It was good experience for Jim too. Charles was constantly correcting the boy while Frank was much more patient and in less of a hurry.

## Chapter
# TWENTY-EIGHT

Elizabeth went to the mailbox every day hoping that there would be a letter from one of her children.

Margaret and her family were dealing with their own issues. There wasn't much of a demand for musicians, most people couldn't afford the tickets to performances. Ben had to take a job with his father in the garment industry, and that wasn't very lucrative either. They sent as much money as they could to Ben's family still in Europe, but the news was grave. They had two children, Mary-Elizabeth and Aaron David. Mary-Elizabeth was four and had already started taking piano lessons. Aaron was two and from his pictures, Elizabeth thought he looked a lot like Maggie at that age. They weren't able to travel to New York so letters and pictures were their only means of correspondence. Hopefully things would get better once the war was over. She worried that they weren't getting enough fresh meat and vegetables in the city.

Emily and Roger were in London and the nightly air raids were a constant worry. Elizabeth didn't read the newspapers because she was afraid of what they might tell her. They hadn't mentioned having children and Elizabeth wasn't sure if Emily would ever want a baby. She was planning on continuing her career as an architect as soon as things got back to normal. Emily wrote her parents faithfully every week. She knew that if they didn't hear from her, they would think the worst. It kept her with them in spirit back home, where things were simpler and easier and it calmed her to spend the time sharing little details of her daily life with her loved ones. Her letters were full of anecdotes about the countryside. She hoped her parents would be able to come to England one day. She knew they would love it there even though it was so different from Colorado.

Mary wrote her mother to tell her how the boys were doing. She had two little ones – George Jr. was five, Franklin Charles was three and she was expecting again. Elizabeth had stayed with her when she had Junior and little Frank, but wasn't sure if she would be able to make the trip to help with this new baby.

She wrote to her daughter, "Mary, I'll try to come be with you when you have the baby, but with the rationing I'm not sure if I'll be able to. If I can get a train to Helena would you or George be able to pick me up?" Elizabeth knew how difficult it was going to be for Mary to deal with a new baby with two busy, rambunctious little boys.

"Of course, we can pick you up in Helena." Mary wrote, George and I have everything caught up here on the ranch and are just sitting here waiting for little "number three" to make an appearance."

When she got to George and Mary's house Elizabeth was swept off her feet by two little cowboys. "Grammy! We've been waiting for you for hours! Did you ride the train? Was it fun? Momma's in the kitchen, she says you're probably hungry. I'm hungry too! Come on in!" Both boys were talking a mile a minute, and jumping around like jack rabbits.

"Hello boys!! My goodness, look at you! You're growing like two weeds! How does your momma keep you in pants and boots?" She knelt on the ground and held them both. They were sturdy little boys and she loved the way their clean little heads smelled. There was just something soothing about the feel of a child in her arms.

Mary came out on the porch. "Mary, you look like you're ready to pop! When did you say this little person is arriving? Looks like it could be any minute!"

"Mom, it is so wonderful to see you! I've missed you so much! I **feel** like I'm going to pop – and the doctor says it should be here this week for sure. How was your trip? Oh, I'm so glad you're here!" She gave her mother a big hug, around her belly. "George, just put Mom's suitcase in the spare room please, I've got it all ready for her."

George kissed his wife on the cheek, patted her stomach and took Elizabeth's suitcase to her room. "Something smells delicious! Let me wrangle these two and get them washed up and I'll help you get dinner on the table. I'm starving!"

"Thank you, George." Elizabeth called as she looked around George and Mary's house. It was neat and clean, but there were no frills. The house was a perfect reflection of Mary's personality. She would rather be outdoors working with the livestock alongside George than being in the house. He helped with the housework and the cooking. - they were a good team.

"Here Mary - sit down and take a load off your feet. You shouldn't have gone to so much trouble. Now, while I'm here, you take it easy and let me help you. Just show me where you keep things and tell me about your routine and I'll take it from there. Have you changed anything from the last time I was here?"

"Ooh, that sounds wonderful! George! I'm a going to be a lady of leisure!"

Sure enough, Mary had little Joseph James two days later. Elizabeth was so busy running after the boys and taking care of the household and Mary that she hardly had time to breathe. She loved the feeling that she was needed, but of course, she was needed at home too. Poor Frank was all alone on the ranch so she couldn't stay too long. As soon as Mary was well enough to handle things on her own, she went home. George and the boys took her to the train, while Mary stayed at home with the baby. "Thank you so much for coming Mom! I miss you already. Write to me as soon as you get home. I love you Momma."

"I love you too Mary. Take care of yourself – don't overdo it and let George help you. He's perfectly capable and is willing to help. Just let him – OK?"

The boys waved as the train pulled away, she said a little prayer, asking God to watch over the little family and keep them safe. They were such good little boys, they were happy and well adjusted, but full of mischief too. "Just the way boys should be", she thought. She was pleasantly tired and was anxious to see her husband. She hoped the war would be over soon and all of her children would be safe and sound.

## Chapter

# TWENTY-NINE

Frank met her at the train station with a bouquet of flowers. "Oh my, these are beautiful, Frank! Thank you so much!" she kissed him and gave him a hug.

"I thought you might like them. When I saw them they made me think of you." He smiled and kissed her back. "How're Mary and the baby? Did the boys wear you out? I'm glad you're home. I'm sure you must be tired, so let's grab a bite to eat at The Skillet before we head for home. What do you think?"

That sounded wonderful to her – she was a lucky woman. She was anxious to get home, but the thought of making a meal and the clean-up afterward was a little overwhelming. "Yes, let's do that! I'm starving!"

They spent the next hour sharing their news – she told Frank all about Mary and her family and he told her about what had been going on while she was gone. There was news about the war – things were moving fast in Europe and the Germans were on the run. They hoped the Japanese wouldn't keep fighting once the Germans surrendered. There was a glimmer of hope that Emily and Joseph might be home soon.

One evening while they listened to the radio, they heard that the U.S. had bombed Hiroshima and that would probably end the war. The U.S. bombed Nagasaki soon after that and the Japanese surrendered. Frank and Elizabeth had no idea what type of bomb was used until much later, but were just happy that the fighting was over. They hugged and laughed and cried with relief.

They continued to get letters from Emily. She wrote telling them that she would be coming back to the States in a couple of months. Her enlistment period was over, but she would be in the Reserves for several more years. "Did you notice that she didn't mention Roger in her letter?" Frank asked.

"Now that you mention it, you're right. I wonder if everything's alright with them."

A few weeks later they got a letter telling them that Emily would be home the next week. Frank and Elizabeth met her at the train station. "There she is! Oh my, doesn't she look smart in that uniform? But she's too thin, I need to feed that girl!"

"Now, Elizabeth don't say anything – just let her be."

"Emily, Emily! Here we are! Oh, we're so glad to see your face! We've missed you so much! Here – let me look at you!" Frank stepped back and let Elizabeth be the first to greet her. Emily smiled at him over her mother's shoulder and then went to hug him too.

"You both look wonderful! How do you do it? You never change! I'm so happy to be here. I can't wait to get to the peace and quiet of home. How're Charlie and his family?"

"They had a problem with one of their calves this morning and couldn't get away. But they'll be at the house when we get there. You won't believe how big Amanda and Jimmy are."

Later, after everyone had eaten and Charles and his family had gone home, Emily and her parents sat in the kitchen just enjoying the quiet. "So, I'm sure you're wondering where Roger is."

"Well, we did notice that he isn't with you."

"Daddy, you're a master of the understatement." She smiled at him. "I don't know what happened, but I think we just spent too much time together under stressful circumstances. You know our entire relationship was too much too fast. So, we've decided to take a break from each other and see how we feel in a couple of months. We still love each other but for right now, we need to heal. The war was a never-ending series of crises and we were both under so much pressure all of the time that we didn't have time for our marriage. We'll just have to see what happens."

"We're sorry to hear this Em, but you know you can stay here for as long as you want or need to." Elizabeth went to sit beside her daughter and held her hand. "Roger's a good man and we hope you two can work this out, but if not, we'll support your decision either way."

"I know that and I appreciate it. I just need a few days to get my head on straight, and then I'm going to Denver to see if I can get my job back. When I left, they told me they would hold my position for me."

"The economy's getting back to normal and I hear that there's a building boom in the cities. I'm sure Denver is no exception. Do you need any money?"

"No, thank you, Daddy, I was able to save enough of my military pay to get back on my feet. I have enough for a few month's rent and living expenses, if I'm careful."

"Well, just let us know if you need anything, OK?"

She stayed with them for a couple of weeks and then decided it was time to go to Denver and try to pick up the pieces of her life. Once again, Elizabeth and Frank stood on the train platform and watched a child leave. They were getting used to this, but it was still hard not to worry.

## Chapter
# THIRTY

Joseph was different. He had a haunted look about him that worried Frank and Elizabeth. He hadn't written to let them know he was coming home, he just showed up in town one day and hitch-hiked to within a couple of miles of the farm. Elizabeth saw a stranger walk down their lane and watched as Lucy ran up to him wagging her tail and jumping around, even though she was an old lady. The stranger knelt down and hugged the dog and Elizabeth knew it was Joe.

She ran out of the house and met him in the lane. "Joe! Why didn't you let us know you were coming? We would have met your train. Oh, you're a sight for sore eyes – I can't believe it's really you! I'm so happy to see you. We've been so worried about you and missed you so much!"

She tried to hug him, but he was stiff as a board.

"Hi Mom, sorry I didn't write, it's been crazy since we landed in San Diego and I just headed toward home. Most people are more than willing to give a sailor a lift so I knew I'd make it sooner or later. Lucy, look at you! You're acting like a puppy! I guess she's glad to see me too." He smiled at his mother, but the smile didn't quite reach his eyes.

"Come on in, I imagine you're hungry. I'll make you some ham and eggs – does that sound good?"

"It sounds more than good. I haven't eaten yet today, I just wanted to get home. Where's Dad?"

"Your father is working the east corn field today. Go put your duffle bag in your room and wash up while I get your breakfast going. It's so good to see you Honey."

Joseph ate like he hadn't had a meal in weeks. Elizabeth kept his plate full until he said, "I can't eat another bite. Thank you, Mom, that was delicious, I've been thinking about your biscuits for days." He'd always liked her biscuits.

"Do you want to take a bath? I've got some warm water on the back of the stove. I was going to do a wash today so I can throw your clothes in too."

"That sounds too good to be true! Yes, here let me fill the tub and thanks for washing my clothes. My pants would just about stand up by themselves they're so dirty. I must look like a hobo or something."

"Well, you look good to me, even with the beard. Take your time, I'll ride out to the field and let your father know you're here."

When Frank saw her coming he pulled over by the road. "Is everything alright?"

"Yes, everything's okay, Joseph just came home."

"What? How did he get home? Where is he?"

"Apparently he hitchhiked from California. He ate breakfast and is at the house getting cleaned up. He looks pretty bad Frank. If Lucy hadn't recognized him, I might not have let him in."

"I'll come home right now. Tell him I'll be there in just a few minutes."

Elizabeth turned the car around and went home. When she went into the house, she found Joe sound asleep in his room. He must have been exhausted. He'd shaved and looked more like her son. He had dark circles under his eyes but his face was more relaxed as he slept. She wondered what the war had done to her boy.

When he woke up and came out of his room Frank was waiting for him. "Dad, it's good to see you. You look good."

"It's good to see you too Son. Your mother and I are happy that you're home. Do you want Charlie and his gang to come over?"

"Not yet. I'm not fit to see anyone just yet. A lot of noise and chatter seems to get to me lately. Maybe in a couple of days, after I get my bearings."

"Of course. We'll just keep it simple and quiet and let you rest for a few days. You look like you had a long trip."

"Longer than I can even tell you. If you don't mind, I think I'll just go out and have a look around the place. I'd like to take old Lucy out for a little walk." He got up from the table and headed out the door, calling to the dog as he left.

He stayed with them for several weeks and little by little the old Joe returned. Frank kept him busy working with the livestock, which he had always enjoyed. They didn't ask him about the war and he didn't offer to tell them. It was something he obviously didn't want to talk about or remember.

At breakfast one morning he said, "I'd like to go back to school and get my veterinary degree. We were told when we mustered out of the Navy that we qualified for the G.I. Bill so I can go to school for nearly nothing."

"That sounds like a good idea Joe. When are you going to leave?"

"I'm going to Denver to see Emily and maybe Yvonne later this week and then I'll go to Ft. Collins to see what I have to do to get back into school."

"Your car is still here in the shed, and is all ready for you. I have a few things I'd like to send to Emily."

Lucy chased after his car as he drove down the lane and once again Frank and Elizabeth waved goodbye to one of their children. This time they were happy to see a much different person leave than the damaged man that had come home to them.

## Chapter
# *THIRTY-ONE*

The years seemed to fly by. President Roosevelt's Rural Electrification Association (The REA) had finally come all the way out to the Sand Hills. Frank and Elizabeth had electricity!! No more wind generator, no more missed programs, and no more kerosene lanterns – they had electric lights! They bought a refrigerator and a washing machine. They replaced the old, hand-operated cream separator and they got a telephone!

Elizabeth wasn't sure she liked the telephone. "I just can't get used to that infernal noise! The thing rings all day long!" They were on an eight-party line and everyone's calls rang on everyone else's phone and every time the phone rang Elizabeth jumped a foot. Each family had their own specific ring. Frank and Elizabeth's ring was – two long rings followed by one short ring. So, every time the phone would ring, she would have to count the number of longs and shorts. And of course, everyone could hear everyone else's conversations. There was no privacy on a party line. In order to make a call they had to wind the crank, then the operator came on the line and they told her who they were trying to reach. Luckily, they lived in a small town so the operator was familiar with nearly everyone's number. The "Twentieth Century" had come to the farm.

Early one morning, Frank was walking toward the house with a bucket of milk in each hand. The next thing he knew, he was down on his knees. He had a terrible pain in his chest. Elizabeth found him in the farm yard in a puddle of milk. "Frank! What's wrong?!?"

She helped him to his feet. "I don't know, I just had this awful pain in my chest that went clear down my arm. I spilled the milk…."

"Oh, for heaven's sake, don't worry about the milk, let's get you into the house. I'm going to call Doc Ralston and get you into town." She was glad she had that telephone and a car. She wished she would have had those things when James got bitten by the rattle snake.

She called the doctor's office and his nurse told them he would meet them at the hospital. They were on their way within five minutes. Of course, by the time they got to town, Charles and Laura were already at the hospital. One of the people on their party line had called Laura to tell her what had happened.

"I don't know what the fuss is all about. I'm fine, it was probably just indigestion."

"Maybe so Mr. Wagner, but it won't hurt to run some tests."

The tests showed that Frank had suffered a severe heart attack. This changed everything for them. The doctor told them that he was at a high risk for another one if he didn't take care of himself.

"I don't know what we should do. I don't feel bad now, but if I'd been on the tractor it could have been even worse." He was sitting up in his hospital bed.

"I know what we're going to do. We're going to sell the farm and move to town. No, don't argue with me. We've got a lot of life ahead of us if we make some changes."

"You know, I've been thinking. Jim is 20 years old, what if we "sold" him the farm. I know he doesn't have any money, but he's a good worker and if we carry the note, I think he'll be able to pay us back in just a few years. That way the place can stay in the family and Charlie is nearby to give him a hand. What do you think of that idea?"

"It sounds like you've been giving this some thought, and I like the fact that the place will stay in the family."

"I was talking to Pete Clemons a few weeks ago. Did you know they've got a couple of lots for sale across from the park? I drove past there the other day. I liked the location. It's close to the library and the hospital."

"I'd like to see it. But, have you been feeling bad and you didn't tell me?"

"Yes, I've been thinking about this, but not because I was feeling bad, but because I'm tired of working all the time and watching you work so hard. We both need a break – you're 70 and I'm 73, so it's time we started living instead of working all of the time. I'd like to travel, maybe even go to England like Emily suggested."

She gave him a hug, "That sounds wonderful, and to tell you the truth I'm ready to do something besides milking cows and dealing with chickens. I'd love to see England and maybe we could even go to Scotland. You know my family is Scottish. Oh, and by the way, I'm only 68!"

"Okay then, let's invite Charles, Laura and Jim over for a chat. There's no point in putting this off any longer than we have to. Are you sure you're 68? You don't look a day over 67!"

Charles and Laura were interested in Frank and Elizabeth's proposal and Jim was ecstatic. He was worried about whether he would be able to take on that much responsibility but knew that he had a good support system with his parents and grand-parents. He had a surprise for them as well. He had been dating Linda Anderson steadily for over a year and wanted to marry her. She was a farm girl and he thought they would make a good team. When Charles and Laura heard this, it seemed to make the decision easier for them.

So, it was decided. Frank and Elizabeth bought both of the lots from Pete Clemons and asked Emily to design a new home for them. She was more than happy to help and within a year they were living in town.

"Just think, Elizabeth, you can walk to the library or downtown and you can get your hair done every week. You might just decide to be a redhead after all!" He winked at her.

"Oh brother – you and your redheads!" she laughed.

Jim and Linda were married in the spring of 1955 and moved onto the farm. The entire family was in favor of their decision to sell the farm to Jim.

Frank and Elizabeth sat on the back porch of their new house and looked over at the city park. They were looking forward to beginning the next chapter in their lives.

## Chapter

# THIRTY-TWO

They loved the house Emily had designed for them. The floor plan flowed well and it was easy to heat and cool. It had a full basement they could use for storage or as a tornado shelter. There were lots of windows and the kitchen was equipped with the latest electric appliances. They had two bathrooms and three bedrooms and hot running water. One of the bedrooms Elizabeth used for her sewing. She still had her treadle machine. "Why don't you get one of those electric sewing machines? It might make sewing a lot easier for you."

"I love my treadle. It reminds me of my mother every time I use it and I'm a lot more comfortable controlling the needle myself." She loved having everything in one place in the cabinets Frank built for the room. She felt like a princess.

They bought furniture for the first time in their married life. The overstuffed couch and chair were comfortable, but Elizabeth preferred her rocker. She'd sit in her chair and reminisce about the nights rocking a sleeping baby and relish the feeling of contentment just sitting and rocking gave her.

The "red bedroom" was for guests. It was a beautiful room and Elizabeth loved it. They called it the "red bedroom" because the vanity bench was upholstered in red fabric. The furniture was light blond ash. The workmanship was fine but she and Frank still kept the bedroom furniture he made for her when they first married.

Emily designed a special space beside the garage for Frank. He could do his wood-working or whatever he wanted without getting sawdust or mud all over the house. It was heated, with plenty of windows and was well lit and he spent most of his time there enjoying his hobbies.

Frank took a lot of pride in his lawn. He made sure there were no weeds and that it was mowed and manicured to perfection. After all he had a reputation as a farmer to uphold. "Elizabeth, do you want to plant tulips in the flower boxes in the front?"

"Yes, I would like that, I would like rose bushes too, and can we plant some flowers by the back porch?

"We can do anything your heart desires and my old back can take. Just let me know where you want to plant things and what colors you want and we'll get them in the ground." Life was good.

Their children were all doing well. Joseph opened a veterinary practice in Sterling, Colorado. It was fifty miles away but they visited him as often as they could. Emily designed his clinic. It was a handsome, efficient building and the layout was well thought out and very functional. Several other vets commissioned her to design similar buildings for them, so it led to more business for her. She had gotten her architectural license and opened her own practice in Denver. Things were difficult at first, but little by little her reputation had grown and she was busy.

Emily and Roger were back together, but Yvonne had met someone while Joe was in the Navy and was married. Emily was too busy with her business to think about having children and Roger seemed okay with that decision. Joseph had a lady friend, but preferred spending time with his animals. Lucy was retired from her herding duties and lived with him. He still had issues left over from the war. It would be called PTSD someday.

Margaret taught music at the school her children attended and Ben played in the New York Symphony Orchestra. They visited

Frank and Elizabeth as often as possible and Frank and Elizabeth went to New York at least once a year to visit them. They wanted to be a part of all of their grand-children's lives. Mary and Margaret's kids all spent a week with Frank and Elizabeth in the summer and then they would all go visit Mary and George. The city kids really loved going to Montana and riding horses – pretending to be cowboys. Frank liked to visit with George, ranching in Montana was different from the way he had run his herd in Colorado. And, of course Elizabeth loved seeing Mary and her brood.

Charles and Laura were busy. Charles bought all of the available land adjacent to his farm and, they hired a full-time ranch hand. Laura returned to teaching when the kids were in high school. Charles was on the school board which was almost a full-time job. Elizabeth remembered how the Schubert's had welcomed her to Hartford so many years ago and wondered if Charles knew how important that school board job was.

Jim and his wife were expecting their first child. Frank and Elizabeth were going to be great-grandparents! Linda called Elizabeth one morning, "Grandma Wagner, you'll never guess what I found in the storage shed! I don't even know why I was poking around in there, but any way, I found a cradle."

The cradle Frank made for Charlie, ah the memories that conjured up! "Oh, Linda that was Jim's father's cradle. Grandpa made that before he was born. Actually, all of the babies slept in that cradle."

"Do you think I can use it for our baby?"

"Why, of course! Grandpa will be pleased to know that his great-grandchild will be sleeping in that cradle." Elizabeth made a mental note to make a new down mattress and coverlet for the little bed.

Amanda was engaged to be married. She went to the teacher's college in Greeley and. would be doing her student teaching in the fall. Her fiancée was a teacher too so they had a lot in common. They hoped to get jobs in the same school, hopefully in Greeley or Ft. Collins. Their future was bright.

Now it was time for Frank and Elizabeth to take it easy and enjoy life. This would take some getting used to – leisure time was a new experience for them - it was another chapter in their lives. That gem was still there but had taken on a new, warm appearance.

# THIRTY-THREE

"Frank, I'm going to the nursing home. I'll be back to make your lunch." Elizabeth volunteered at the local nursing home two days a week. She read to the residents, or helped them with their correspondence, or just visited with them. It made her feel useful. Frank volunteered at the county museum. The feed and grain store where they used to take their cream and eggs had been turned into a museum. Frank had lived in the county most of his eighty-five years and knew a lot about the history of the area. He'd even donated some of his old farming implements for the "Advances in Farming" exhibit.

"Ok I'll be here when you get back, be careful crossing the street, remember you turned your ankle last week."

"Isn't he ever going to let me forget that?" she thought. "Oh well, at least he still cares about me, or at least he cares about my ankle!"

Frank and Elizabeth had become fixtures in town in the twelve years they lived there. Every year on the Saturday after Thanksgiving the town had their own version of the Macy's parade, and the star of the show was Santa Claus, of course. Frank started letting his beard grow in early September so it would be long enough for him to be a convincing Santa by the time of the parade. He had been Santa Claus for quite a few years and Elizabeth dressed up as Mrs. Claus.

They rode down the main street of town, Interocean Avenue, in an open wagon that Jim pulled with Frank's little garden tractor. They waved and threw candy to all the kids along the parade route. This year there was a sign on the side of their wagon "Thank You for Your Votes! Mayor Charlie Wagner!!"

Santa's main job was to turn the Christmas lights on at each of the businesses along the way and then turn on the lights on the big Christmas tree in the courthouse square. Later they would go downstairs in the courthouse and the little ones would sit on Frank's lap and tell him what they wanted for Christmas. Elizabeth helped get the littlest ones up on Santa's lap. This year it was really cold and Frank was shivering by the time they got to the courthouse.

"Santa! You've got the same boots as my dad! Mom, Mom, look – Santa must shop at Sears Roebuck too! He's got the same boots that Daddy has!" Everyone thought that was pretty funny. Frank made a mental note to get some different boots before next year. He liked to make his costume look as realistic as possible.

A couple of days later Frank came down with a cold. He had gotten chilled during the parade and some of the little ones that sat on his lap had runny noses and colds. "I feel pretty sick. Can you take my temperature? My head and chest hurt." He rarely complained so she was a little worried.

Elizabeth felt his forehead, he was hot. "Here, open your mouth and put this under your tongue. You probably picked something up when you were playing Santa." Sure enough he had a fever. She gave him some aspirin and lots of water and tried to make him comfortable. "Do you want me to call Doc Ralston?"

"No, I'll be alright. It's just a cold. I just need to rest. Some chicken noodle soup might be nice though...."

"Okay, chicken noodle soup coming right up. It's canned but it should make you feel better." She made him some soup and he fell asleep in his chair when he was finished.

When she got back from the nursing home he was still asleep in his chair and he was still feverish. He didn't want to see the doctor so she took care of him at home, but he wasn't getting any better.

"Okay, enough is enough. We're going to the doctor. You've been sick for a week and you're getting worse."

"Alright, I think you're right. I can't seem to kick this."

The fact that he was willing to go to the doctor scared her. She called and the nurse told her to come in, they would make room for him. She heard something in Elizabeth's voice that let her know this was serious.

They went in to the examining room and waited for the doctor. "Gee, I feel awful. My head's pounding and I can't seem to get my breath."

A new, young doctor had just arrived in town to work in the newly constructed hospital. He listened to Frank's chest, "Mr. Wagner we need to get you into the hospital. Your lungs sound like you've got pneumonia. With your history of heart issues we'd better be safe than sorry."

"Okay Doc, whatever you say." That wasn't like Frank. She'd expected him to resist having to stay in the hospital.

They got him settled in a room and she called Charles. "Your father is sick. I took him to the doctor and they think he's got pneumonia. He's in the hospital in Room 25."

"Okay, we'll be right there, Mom. Are you okay?"

"Yes I'm fine, but I'm really worried about your dad."

By the time Charles and Laura got to the hospital, Frank was worse. He wasn't responsive and he was on oxygen.

"My god Mom, how long has he been sick?"

"He got sick right after the parade. We thought it was just a cold."

Elizabeth spent the night in Frank's hospital room. His breathing was labored and she unconsciously tried to breathe for him. She held his hand and every time he took a breath, she willed him to take the next one. She just dozed off when the machine he was attached to started to beep. The nurses came in right away to check on him.

One ran out of the room and called the doctor. By the time the doctor got there, the machine had stopped beeping and Frank had stopped breathing.

"I'm so sorry Mrs. Wagner. I'm afraid there was nothing we could do. Your husband has passed away. Is there anyone we can call?"

"No! No! He just has a cold! Frank!" She leaned over his bed and held him in her arms. "Please wake up! Please don't leave me!"

They had called Charles and he and Laura got there shortly after his father passed away. "Dad! Mom! What's happened? Oh Mom,"

Laura wrapped her arms around Elizabeth. "Mother Wagner, here let me hold you. Is there anything I can do for you?"

Elizabeth couldn't talk, she had just lost the love of her life, her other half. What would she do without Frank?

All of the kids came home for the funeral. Their grief was palpable. Everyone that knew him respected and liked Frank Wagner. He would be sorely missed. Several people spoke at his service. His family hadn't known what a pillar of the community their father had been. Elizabeth knew, she had always known what a wonderful man her husband was.

Frank was buried at the cemetery next to little Jimmy's grave. She felt that at least James wouldn't be alone any more now that Frank was there with him.

She was alone. How could she go on? This was a chapter she didn't think she could take. The glow in that gem was gone.

Chapter

# THIRTY-FOUR

The great-grandchildren were her saving grace. Jim's little ones came to visit her every day and she looked forward to their visits. "Grammy! Look what I made in school today! It's a picture of a house and a tree and a dog and a cat! It's for you to put on your "frigadator." Jim's second son Charlie was in kindergarten.

"Oh my, it's beautiful! You did a very nice job on the tree, and I see you put an apple in it. Where are the people? Does your house have any people?"

"No, it's a house for cats and dogs. I should have put a bird in the tree. I'll do that next time." He reached for a magnet on her fridge and put his picture under it. He reminded her so much of Charles when he was little.

"It's "RE FRIG ER AT OR" Silly." James Jr., was in the second grade and was quiet and more serious.

"Jimmy, how're you doing? Do you have a lot of homework? How did you do on that spelling test today?"

"I'm good. I have math homework and I got a B+ on my test. I'm hungry, Grandma, do you have anything to eat?"

"Yes, there should be some cookies in the cookie jar, but ask your mother if you can have one. You don't want you to spoil your dinner."

173

"Mom, can we have a cookie? Please?"

"Yeah, Mom can we have a cookie? PLEEESE?"

"Cookie!" Linda sat at the table and held Laura Ilene on her lap. Linda had her hands full with the two boys and the toddler.

"Yes, you can each have one cookie and give one to your sister too. We brought you some lasagna for your dinner Grandma Wagner. Hope you like it."

"Thank you Linda, I love lasagna, it smells really good! How're things on the farm? Has the snow melted?"

"Would you like to take a ride out to the farm? I can take you out there any time you want."

"No, I'm not ready to go down that road yet. Maybe in a couple of months. We'll see."

After Linda and the children left, Elizabeth sat down to eat her dinner. She didn't have much of an appetite but knew she should eat something. It was lonely without Frank. She found herself talking to him as though he was there with her sometimes. "I think I must be going crazy! I hope nobody hears me talking to myself! Elizabeth, you have to get a grip on yourself or they're going to put you in the loony bin!!"

A few months later, Elizabeth began to pick up the pieces of her life. She helped at the nursing home again and even started volunteering at the museum. She knew a few things about the area too. "Life goes on", she thought.

## Chapter

# THIRTY-FIVE

And her life did go on. She kept busy and her family made sure she wasn't alone. She visited Margaret and her family in New York. She found that she actually liked the city with all of its sights and sounds – but for short periods of time. After awhile the hustle and bustle got a bit overwhelming. She craved the quiet of her little town.

She especially liked to visit Mary on the ranch. The boys were lively and energetic. There was never a dull moment. They were either trying to ride the goats or chasing the geese or fishing in the horse trough. They put on their own rodeos in the corral and as Elizabeth watched, she worried that they would break an arm or a leg. She enjoyed the commotion for a while but then needed to go back to the peace and quiet of her own home.

Her visits to Emily in Denver were wonderful. Emily's house was a show place and Elizabeth had her own guest suite. They went to concerts and plays and ate at trendy places. The three of them would take drives up into the foothills to see the beautiful scenery. She still loved the mountains. It was quiet and relaxing but interesting. There was always something new and exciting to do and see, but after a while she just wanted to be back in her own little spot in the world.

Joseph was always happy to have her visit, but she knew it was difficult for him to entertain her, so she would stop in for a few hours when she went to Sterling to shop. It worked well for both of them.

When she got back from her visits she would go to the cemetery and tell Frank all about them. "You would have loved…" or "You should have seen…." Or, "I miss you so much…." The gem was becoming dimmer and dimmer.

It was 1972. 88-year-old Elizabeth Ilene Ross Wagner was finally ready to go. She had seen so many changes in the world during her life. Frank had been gone for five years. She brushed her hair and laid down on the bed she had shared with her husband for so many years. She closed her eyes and waited for him to come for her.

"Are you ready now?"

"Yes, Frank," she held out her hand, "I've missed you so much and I have so much to tell you. Where are the others?"

# ABOUT THE AUTHOR

Cheryl grew up listening to her mother and both grand-mothers talk about their experiences of life on the remote Colorado prairie. While not everything here is real, their stories as well as those of their friends, about the trials and triumphs of their lives were inspiring and she wanted to both honor them and share their memories.

CPSIA information can be obtained
at www.ICGtesting.com
Printed in the USA
LVHW101726300523
748294LV00003B/274

9 781489 730817